Perfect Picture

THE SHADOWDANCE CLUB 7

ShadowDance Club

AVERY GALE®

Dedication

To everyone who has been given a second chance at love and understands what an incredible gift they've been given.

Chapter 1

The soul never thinks without a picture.
—Aristotle

ILAINA RED CLOUD sat at the table with her brothers and their new wife, surrounded by friends and family, wondering how she could feel so alone. Her emotions might have been in a dark place, but she knew from experience, her smile was bright and easily masked the emptiness currently torturing her soul. Ilaina was over the moon her three older brothers had found Layla. She and her new sister-in-law had become fast friends, and Ilaina was equally thrilled she was going to be an aunt in a few months.

Known as Lainy to her family and friends, Ilaina had only recently moved back to her childhood home in Climax, Colorado. She credited the move to her desire to start her own advertising and marketing company, but there was a darker, much more menacing reason underlying the move that had been much more pressing.

Lainy's real motivation to move home had more to do with the unintended consequence of the years she'd spent with her face gracing the covers of nearly every magazine in the free world. All the attention her years as a super-model had garnered her more than a few obsessive fans and several crazy-assed followers.

The latest cyber-stalker she'd picked up had only been an inconvenience in the beginning, but his comments seemed to shift about six months ago. The communication continued to become more and more possessive, and if she'd learned one thing over the years, it was that your security staff had no personal stake in your safety. Staff only protects you because you are paying them an exorbitant amount of money, and their dedication is rarely proportionate to their salary.

The other thing she'd learned was, that in the end, it didn't matter how good your security staff was or how many times you reached out to law enforcement, the bottom line—there was very little you could do to keep people with bats in their belfries at a safe distance. Lainy didn't consider herself paranoid, but she'd come to the conclusion "Crazy 4U" had given himself an apt nickname.

Glancing around her, Lainy noted even though she'd just started building friendships with the women currently sitting around the table, she enjoyed their diverse backgrounds and wacky senses of humor. Layla seemed to have fit in quickly despite having to deal with a boatload of personal and family issues over the years as well... her new sister-in-law was one of the best examples of resilience Lainy had ever seen. Giving herself a mental slap to regain her focus, Lainy realized the seat next to her that had been empty was now occupied by Alex Lamont.

"Do you mind if I sit here, Ilaina?" Alex Lamont was a former Navy SEAL and along with his twin brother Zach, was married to the little blonde package of dynamite at the other end of the table. Katarina Lamont must have seen the hesitance on Lainy's face because she looked at her and smiled before nodding her head in Alex's direction as if encouraging her to talk to him. *Damn, this isn't going anywhere good, I just know it. Alex doesn't do social chit-chat.*

"No, not at all. How have you been, Alex?" Smiling at him, she tried to keep her tone even, so she didn't give away her unease. "Cash tells me you stay pretty busy with various business interests and three small children."

Lainy knew more than that but not much more. She'd known there had been several times recently her oldest brother, Cash had worked on contract missions for the Lamonts, but he hadn't shared any of the details with her. She and Cash had always been incredibly close despite their seven-year age difference, and she was grateful they'd made the effort to stay in close contact with each other despite often finding themselves on opposite sides of the globe.

Even when he'd still been a SEAL, her brother had never left the country without at least leaving her a message, telling her what little he could. Admittedly, that wasn't much if anything most of the time, but it had always made her feel good to know he'd made the effort to ensure she knew how much he loved her each and every time he'd gone out.

Alex's soft laughter brought her back to the moment.

"He's right, and truthfully, I have no idea how any man can pull it all off alone. It takes Zach and I both to manage the lot of them. I shudder to think what it would be like to try to keep Katarina in line without his help, let alone the children." His smile took the sting out of his words.

Lainy was well aware of how much the man sitting in front of her cherished his sweet wife. Alex and Zach Lamont could have easily followed in their mother's footsteps and had successful modeling careers. Both men were incredibly handsome with bodies well-toned by their years in the military. She knew they fielded calls from various agencies while they'd been in school with her brothers, but the U.S. Navy SEALS had been their dream, and their desire to serve their nation had never been in question.

He sat in silence for a couple of minutes, but then she felt the energy around them shift as he turned to her. The look on his face told her he was finally going to get to the point.

"Ilaina, I wanted to apologize to you. I'm sorry I had to call Noah away from your date the other night." When she started to speak, he held up his hand and shook his head, so she just sat back and waited. "I promise you, I knew full well how incredibly important that evening was to Noah, and if I had had any other option, I would have used it. But the truth is, a young girl's future was hanging in the balance, and Noah was the only person I could count on to get in under the radar and help her."

Lainy found herself watching Alex intently as he spoke. She could see he was trying to walk a very fine line between revealing enough to appease her and still respecting some unseen boundary he'd previously set for the conversation. Whether it was the privacy of the girl he'd spoken about or something to do with Noah, Lainy wasn't sure. Noticing she was shredding the napkin in her hand, Lainy purposefully stilled her hands and took a deep breath before responding.

"Alex, I appreciate you taking time to speak with me, but really, it's okay. The history between Noah and myself is… well, it's complicated." She didn't want to rehash the old hurts, after all, this night was supposed to be a celebration, and she'd already been feeling a bit disconnected. Discussing old wounds wouldn't be in anyone's best interest tonight… or ever if anyone asked her.

"But that's precisely the point—it does matter because that wasn't the first time it's happened. A large part of your complicated history is because of another call I made to Noah several years ago, another time when his unique ability was needed to help a group of young women. He packed up in the middle of the night and went then as well." Alex was looking at the table where his finger had been slowly tracing figure eights in the condensation from a cup, but when he slowly lifted his gaze to hers, she was shocked to see the regret and grief reflected in their dark depths.

After several long seconds, Alex finally spoke again, this time his voice was laced with a hesitance she would have never associated with him. Usually, Alex Lamont was the epitome of controlled self-assurance, so his hesitance made her pay particular attention.

"I don't ask for favors very often, Ilaina, but I'm going to ask you for one. Please listen carefully to what Noah has to say. He is not the person you believe him to be, and the night he left your bed, it was because our team needed him, and because of his unselfish actions, we were able to rescue a group of young ladies who are alive and back with their families. The ripples of his kindness and sacrifice have stretched far and wide, I assure you."

She was shocked by what he'd said, not only because he'd asked her for a favor, but she had known Alex Lamont her entire life, and she'd never seen him look or sound as vulnerable as he did right now. She was also familiar with the types of missions his team favored, so it was easy to imagine them being involved in a rescue since the Lamonts were well known for that sort of mission. They'd interrupted several human trafficking operations she knew about since the foreign press didn't feel any obligation to hide the identities of U.S. operatives. She'd read about their daring rescues more than once.

If Noah was involved with those missions, he was likely involved in some of the more intensely gray areas Cash had also mentioned they often dealt with. Why a photographer would play an essential role in any of those missions was certainly an interesting question.

Lainy had known the entire Lamont family for as long as she could remember, and if there was one thing she knew about them, it was they were intensely loyal. Honesty and integrity were tenets they lived by. Taking a deep breath, she sighed, then nodded.

"I promise to listen, Alex, but that doesn't mean I'm going to change my mind. After all, he's had opportunities to tell me and hasn't taken them. Why would his explanations be any more relevant now than they would have been before?" She'd tried to keep the hurt from her voice, but from the tightening of Alex's jaw, she feared she'd failed as miserably.

Alex Lamont and his brother were mirror image twins, but Lainy had never had any trouble telling them apart. Their personalities had always made them appear very different in her opinion, and the thoughtful, intense man sitting next to her was most definitely a Dominant. She'd grown up in a house filled with men just like Alex so she could spot them at a thousand paces. Alex was leading her in this conversation, she knew it but couldn't seem to muster the energy to battle with him.

After years of butting her head against the wall, she'd learned to choose her battles with Doms carefully. They were masters at manipulating situations, so they were the ones asking questions and experts in steering even the most casual conversation exactly where they wanted it to go. He surprised her when he leaned close and looked deeply into her eyes.

"Let me ask you this, Ilaina. If you wanted to hurt Cash, Collin, or Clay, what would you do?"

She was taken aback by the question at first but then saw where he was heading. When she answered truthfully, "Hurt Layla," he nodded his head.

"That's right. Noah has known all along if the wrong people found out about his interest in you, they would exploit it. He couldn't risk endangering you, and he was wise enough to know he'd be much less effective if his Achilles heel were exposed." Alex looked longingly down the table at his wife, then returned his attention to Ilaina.

"Keep in mind, sometimes, good people do the wrong things for all the right reasons." With those words, he stood and looked down at her. "All I ask is you listen. I owe him, hell, a lot of people owe him, and we'd like to see him find some of the happiness he's given others." He turned and walked away without looking back, and Lainy was left staring at his back as he made his way back to his brother and wife.

Lainy hadn't seen or heard from Noah since he cut short their date almost three weeks earlier. She'd been more than a little surprised he hadn't tried to contact her, but she had been busy enough helping with the plans for her brothers and Layla's wedding, she hadn't really spent much time considering the consequences of his absence either. Just as she was sitting back against her seat, she heard Kat squeal and saw grins spread over the faces of each of the women sitting around the over-sized table. Katarina Lamont was instantly on her feet, moving toward the dance floor, pulling her friends along with her.

Jenna grabbed Lainy's hand. "Come on, girlfriend. No one escapes Kat's fun. She's a big Kenny Chesney fan, so I'm sure this song is no accident." Lainy realized, "Guitars & Tiki Bars" was playing, and from the look of the dance floor, every woman in the place was going to be rocking right along with Kat.

Lainy laughed and let the music carry her along. She quickly got into the carefree lyrics and Caribbean beat. God, she loved the freedom she found when she was dancing... she always had. It was one of the things she'd always had in common with her oldest brother. Cash taught her to dance when she'd been in grade school, and he was still her favorite dance partner.

Lainy was having a great time with her new friends. They were all hooting and hollering... lost in the music and the joy of the night's celebration. God in heaven, she'd forgotten how great it was to have friends. After spending the last several years traveling the world and having her picture taken in every conceivable exotic locale, she was still trying to shake the feeling of isolation all those motel rooms had instilled in her.

The music transitioned to Kenny Chesney's "Pirate Flag," and the dancing got exponentially sexier until it was bordering on obscene. Lainy laughed as the Doms in their group suddenly seemed to position themselves around the dance floor. Laughing to herself, she wondered if they were attempting to erect a force field to shield the carefree souls heating up the floor. It was likely the Doms among them wanted to discourage any men outside their circle from watching their women gyrating to the pulsing beats of the music. The margaritas she'd had earlier were finally taking the edge off her unease. She was able to let herself fall completely under the spell cast by the bonds of friends and family.

Moving to the edge of the floor as the song ended, she was laughing with Tori Bartell and Layla. Turning to exit the dance floor, Lainy came face to face with Noah Drummond. He pulled her into his arms and leaned down, nuzzling his nose against the sensitive place behind her ear. She heard him suck in a deep breath as if he could inhale her deep inside himself, and rather than feeling her usual urge to put distance between them, Lainy's body pressed closer to him on instinct.

"Dance with me, *Cara*."

Moving around the dance floor in perfect harmony as if they'd been dancing together forever, she laughed to herself because she could now see how easily Alex had set her up. Oddly enough, knowing Alex had set the stage for Noah's arrival didn't annoy her at all, she wasn't even sure right now why it should have. Listening to Keith Whitley's "Don't Close Your Eyes" as Noah moved her around the floor, she felt like he was taking her on an entirely different musical ride and didn't it just figure the man would show up just as the song she'd always considered *pure sex set to music* was queued to play.

"I remembered you loved this song, *Cara*. I asked them to play it for us. I wanted to hold you against me while the words wrapped around you. Watching you dance when I first walked in reminded me how much I loved dancing with you. God, baby, the music loves your body. It caresses your soul, and your body answers with movements so sensual, I couldn't take my eyes off you. I'm glad I called ahead to ask for this song to be ready because there is only one thing better than feeling you pressed close while we move as one around the floor." He didn't need to explain what trumped dancing because sex with Noah had been more than a physical act with mutual benefits—making love with him had been a sensual experience that always touched her soul. Lainy now understood the underlying sense of urgency she'd felt while Alex had been talking to her, he'd obviously known Noah was on his way.

Her dads had always told her there would be times in life when you have to decide if a situation was a battlefield worth dying on, and at this moment, it wasn't even a question—so she let herself settle against his strength and for once... she planned to let go and enjoy the feel of being held in his arms. She let the music seduce her and let him lead her in a dance that quickly turned in to something much more intimate. The energy all around her suddenly seemed to become charged with raw desire, or maybe she was just projecting her feelings onto those around her because she'd been alone for so long.

Chapter 2

NOAH HAD TRAVELED around the world—several times, in fact, but he'd never met anyone else whose soul called to him the way Ilaina Red Cloud's did—it was if the deepest parts of them spoke a language only the other could hear.

When he first entered her family's new dance club, his gaze immediately zeroed in on her. Seeing the carefree way she danced with the other women had stolen his breath. Watching as she lost herself in the music, he felt an almost magnetic pull leading him directly to the edge of the dance floor. He instinctively knew where he needed to be and watched in wonder as she let the music and her friends sweep her up in the joy around them. She was always so guarded, it was pure magic to see her step out from behind the wall she'd built so carefully around her heart.

The picture he'd taken of her—that night so long ago—was the only other time he'd seen clear to the soul of the woman hidden behind the glass wall shielding her from the rest of the world. He always likened it to thick blocks of ice—you could see the beautiful woman on the other side, but you couldn't touch her. Noah wasn't sure why that wall was in place, but he planned to blast it with wave after wave of heat until he melted it once and for all.

Ilaina Red Cloud was pure poetry in motion as she

moved to the music. The artist in him saw lines of pure perfection in her movements, and the pictures were painted in his mind as fast as his senses could take in the information. He had always known her deep eroticism was probably rooted deep in her DNA, but there was something almost spiritual about the way her mind seemed hyperaware of her body's position at all times. Noah always believed Ilaina's Native American heritage was a much larger part of who she was than even she realized.

As he watched her, Noah felt another presence close at his side, and a quick glance told him it was Ilaina's grandmother. The older woman smiled.

"Return your gaze to the one who holds your heart but lend me your ears for a moment. I will help you all I can, but in the end, your success depends on your ability to protect her. You'll not only face the one who has trampled her trust and frightened her but the shadows that are chasing you as well."

When her words registered, he turned to question her, but she was already gone.

Smiling to himself, he remembered the stories he'd heard about the tiny woman many believed to be one of the strongest *spirit talkers* to have lived in many generations of a culture known for gifted people. He made a mental note to ask Níyol Red Cloud to pose for him—there was a special spiritual essence that surrounded her he wanted to try to capture on film.

When they'd all been kids, Noah had loved listening to the Red Cloud siblings talk about the woman whose name literally translated to *wind*. Cash, Collin, and Clay had laughed as they told their friends she had sworn she'd been named after the wind that spoke to her. While they hadn't taken her words to heart, there had always been a part of

Noah that knew the woman's words were spoken in truth, just as he felt the truth of her words today.

Nodding to the DJ, Noah stepped forward as the music was winding down, and Ilaina was moving to the edge of the floor. Pulling her into his arms was the best feeling in the entire world and feeling her relax against his chest as their bodies moved with the rhythm of the music felt like a prelude to sex as he hoped it was. For some reason, sex with Ilaina Red Cloud had never seemed like the *end*, but merely a *means* to connect with the turbulent soul she kept hidden from the world.

"*Cara*, everything about you fills me, your body pressed against mine, the smell of citrus and sage that surrounds you, and the soft sighs you make when you let yourself become lost in the moment. Come home with me when your family's celebration ends. Let me show you what I wanted to share with you the night I was called away." He felt her stiffen before he spoke again. "I want to talk to you, please, listen to what I have to say."

Noah pulled back just enough that he could look into her obsidian eyes. They reflected so much uncertainty, he wondered if she would agree. When she simply nodded, his knees nearly buckled in relief. He'd traveled for almost thirty-six straight hours to get here for this celebration. He had known she would be here because it was an important occasion for her family. He understood the significance of reestablishing their relationship when she was with her family was critical because the people she loved would be the key to the success or failure of his plan.

"Thank you, *Cara*. There is one more song I want you to listen to as we move around the floor. Listen to the words and think about the possibilities. Some of John Denver's music has become cliché, and that's a shame because he had a unique understanding of the human spirit's fragility most people never grasp."

He'd chosen two songs and had asked the DJ to dedicate this second one to *all* the people celebrating love tonight. As the man spoke the words over the loudspeakers, Noah kissed Ilaina on the forehead, pulled her against his chest, and slid his hand to that sensitive spot just above her ass, pressing her against his hard cock. "Perhaps Love" wafted through the air, and he heard women throughout the room let out a collective sigh, so obviously he wasn't the only one who appreciated the depth of the song's meaning.

"Let the words settle over you as you take them into your heart, *Cara*. Look at the other couples on the floor. See how they understand the strength found in overcoming the obstacles life throws in love's path. They have all endured and flourished because their commitment to each other has seen them through." He didn't want to say too much but wanted to be sure the groundwork had been laid. Swaying to the music, Noah could almost hear her mind processing the lyrics.

Noah wasn't sure exactly what happened to bring Ilaina home, but he knew the woman was much more complicated than the simple business plan reason she'd thrown out to her colleagues in the fashion world. He'd been singing the lyrics softly against her ear, but now whispered.

"I want you to promise that when you find yourself in times of trouble, the song speaks of, and you feel the most alone, you'll remember to let the memory of love bring your heart back to mine. I want you to feel at home in my embrace, *Cara*." He'd bent so he could speak against the soft shell of her ear and was pleased when he felt her whole body shudder. At that moment, he knew instinctively that his suspicions had been correct.

What are you running from Cara? Whatever or whoever it is, we'll face it together. I'll never let anything or anyone hurt you.

As the song ended, he stopped at the edge of the floor near where her brothers were saying their goodbyes to the friends gathered around them. Leaning close, he whispered, "Enjoy your family and say your goodbyes. When you are ready, I'll be waiting for you at the bar. I'll always be waiting, *Cara*." Gently turning her, he leaned down and tenderly bit the spot where her neck met her shoulder.

"*Always, Cara.*"

LAINY STOOD ROOTED in place for several seconds after Noah walked away. When she finally came back to the moment, she looked up and saw Alex watching her thoughtfully. When he simply nodded once and returned his attention to Katarina, Lainy knew it was his way of telling her he felt she was on the right path. For the first time in a long time, she felt as if perhaps she was getting nearer the point in her life when the people and things she surrounded herself with might actually fill her soul rather than drain it.

So often, she'd reflected back on a vacation her family had taken when she was a young girl. On their way back to Colorado, her parents had driven through a small town in Kansas that was a haven for the Amish community. Lainy had been a teenager, and when they'd stopped at a bakery in a small town called Yoder, she'd tried to take a picture of a small boy sitting in a horse-drawn carriage. The boy's father had stopped her, explaining that photographs "steal the soul." She never forgot his words, and even as she'd become one of the most photographed women in the world, each click of the camera had pushed her understanding of his words deeper into her soul.

When she hugged Cash goodbye, she couldn't hold back her tears. She really was incredibly happy for the brother who had always been her knight, champion, guardian, confidant, and best friend.

"Big brother, there are no words to tell you how thrilled I am for you. You deserve each and every moment of happiness that is now yours. You are going to be an amazing husband and father. If I don't see you before you leave on your trip tomorrow, just remember a little piece of my heart goes with you always."

She pulled him down and kissed him on the cheek, then added, "And don't forget to bring me something." Those exact words were something she had said to him every time he called to say he was leaving on a mission… it was an unspoken understanding between them that it was her way of saying "come back to me."

"You are a brat, but I love you more than you'll ever know. Thank you for all you've done for Layla. Your kindness toward her is the greatest gift you have ever given any of us." He hugged her, then turned her to her middle brother, Collin.

"Ilaina, I know you have always been closer to Cash and Clay, but I want you to know, I'm going to work extra hard when we get back to make sure you and I have a chance to make up for lost time. Thank you for everything, I am more grateful than you know that our child will have you for his or her aunt." Collin's hug was almost brutal in its intensity, and she felt the emotion he'd obviously been trying so desperately to hold in check.

When he turned to her youngest brother, Clay, she saw the fun-loving cowboy they all knew and loved. He had always reminded her so much of Dad Julian, and even more so now because she had seen him bring laughter and joy into a situation at just the right moment with Layla, just as the youngest of her dads had always done for their mother.

Growing up with parents involved in a polyamorous marriage had been a blessing beyond anything anyone could ever imagine. All four of the Red Cloud children had been loved unconditionally by all four of their parents, and she couldn't imagine having grown up any other way. Even though the issue of blood parent had never been discussed, it had always been easy to see which of the fathers had sired each of her brothers. Ilaina had always been the DNA enigma as far as she could see because she seemed to have gotten traits from her mother and each of her fathers.

Ilaina was thrilled her three brothers were carrying on the family tradition by finding a woman to share. A poly-marriage had never been her dream, but she knew it had always been theirs, so she was glad Layla had entered their lives. Clay gave her a hug and whispered in her ear.

"You are beautiful both inside and out, little sister. I hope you find the happiness we've found. Please remember, even if it doesn't look exactly like what you thought it would, you shouldn't let it go. Hold on to it with everything in you because you deserve it." She felt the tears start again partly because she wasn't used to such heartfelt words from her "fun" brother, but also because it was almost as if his timing was a message in itself.

Turning to her new sister-in-law, she hugged her tightly.

"I'm so blessed to have you for a sister. I hope to all that is holy my hellion brothers know what a gift they've been given. I'll see you soon. Take care of my little niece or nephew while you are island hopping." And then almost before she and Layla had stopped giggling, her brothers whisked their bride away.

Sighing to herself, she suddenly realized having the house all to herself for the next three weeks didn't seem nearly as appealing now as it had a couple of weeks ago. She'd lived alone for years, but these past few weeks with her family surrounding her had been blissful. For the first time in a long time, she felt safe.

Before she could stop them, she felt the tears spill over her lower lids, and warm arms encircled her from behind. She turned into Noah's warm embrace and rested her cheek against his solid chest. Telling herself it would be alright to let him hold her just this once, she relaxed against him and let herself rely on someone else's strength for the first time in a very long time.

Chapter 3

STANDING AT THE end of the long, polished wood bar, Noah watched the scene play out between Ilaina and her brothers. He couldn't hear what they were saying to her, but it was easy to see she was skating closer and closer to an emotional edge. Each of her brothers brought something different into her life. Noah had always understood the unique bond Ilaina had with her brothers and admired their ability to bring out different sides of her personality.

Watching her get closer and closer to emotional overload was sweet torture. He knew how important it was for them to have this moment, but it was also incredibly difficult to watch her struggle. Even as a kid, he had known she always prided herself on her ability to stay calm as storms raged around her, so he knew becoming emotional in public was going to take a toll on his sweet *Cara*. Hell, from the stories he'd heard from other photographers, her ability to stay the course in the midst of the chaos that surrounded most shoots was almost legendary.

When he noticed the small tells that others who didn't know her as well might have missed, he didn't hesitate to move closer. He meant it when he said he'd always be there for her—he'd always be waiting with his arms and heart open. The fact she was letting him shelter her now told him how unsettled she really was. Moving her to the dance floor, he was glad to hear a slow song come over the speakers.

"Dance with me, *Cara*. Holding you in my arms will be good for both of us." She didn't answer him, but he hadn't expected her to, he just moved her with gentle precision around the floor. It was a testament to her dancing skill that she was able to follow without making any effort to concentrate on the steps.

When they danced their way to the backside of the dance floor, out of sight of her parents and grandmother, he pulled her to the side and tilted her chin up until he could look into her beautiful dark eyes.

"God in heaven, you are absolutely luminous. I swear you get more beautiful each time I see you. It radiates from inside you and draws others to you in a way surface beauty would never be able to." Leaning down he pressed his lips against her. It wasn't a chaste kiss, but it wasn't the soul-deep claiming he'd have rather given her either. "Are you okay, my sweet *Cara*?" When the tears spilled over again, he gently wiped them from her cheeks with his thumbs. She took a deep breath and nodded.

"Yes, or at least I will be. I don't understand why I am so emotional. I'm not usually like this at all. I don't like feeling weak and appearing needy. It just isn't who I am."

He didn't doubt for a moment she was confused by her feelings of vulnerability. What she didn't seem to under-stand was everyone had a breaking point, and he suspected she'd been dangerously close to hers for a while but hadn't felt safe enough to let go.

Noah believed even the strongest person would even-tually reach a point when he or she had been strong for as long as their body and mind could hold up against the current battering them before their last bit of control was swept away like a raging river breaching a levee. He'd seen it happen again and again when a friend or acquaintance finally reached their saturation point or when they eventually found themselves in a place they felt safe enough to let go, the back-surge of emotion was often overwhelming. Noah had always considered himself a student of human behavior for many reasons. Often, during his undercover work of the past decade, that knowledge had meant the difference between life and death.

"Baby, there are a thousand reasons you might be feeling emotional, but the *why* isn't at all important. The only thing that matters is that I want you to know you are always safe with me... just be who you are, *Cara*." He paused for a moment to let his words sink in before continuing. "Let yourself feel, sweetness, and know I will always catch you if you fall over the edge." He placed a soft kiss on her forehead, then smiled at her as she laid her cheek against his chest again. That small sign of her growing trust made his heart swelling with hope.

"Are you ready to go, *Cara*?" He wrapped his arms around her again, sheltering her in his embrace, but he didn't move back on the dance floor.

He barely heard her whispered "Yes," then pulled her back and smiled at her as he looked into her soulful eyes.

"Let's get your things. Did you drive here?" When she shook her head, he was relieved. Truthfully, he didn't want her driving when she was feeling so fragile and distracted. This was also the perfect excuse to have her in his care. He could hardly wait to lift her up into his tall truck and lean across her to fasten her seatbelt—he'd waited years for these moments and wasn't going to miss one single opportunity to be close to her.

After leaving Red Clouds Dancing, they made the short drive to his loft and gallery. He'd been thrilled when Alex and Zach were able to help him secure the purchase of the old mill. The enormous building was a cavernous warehouse that had been empty for years, so he had been able to buy it for a great price. It was structurally sound, and the renovations had been easy since the interior had been open for the most part.

He particularly loved the hidden underground entrance with its remote-controlled doors. Having the garage entrance on the back side of the building had been a big selling point. There was also a second hidden entrance he'd be willing to bet fewer than five people in the entire world knew existed. Finding that feature had been like uncovering a hidden treasure. When Noah had discovered the small railway tunnel hidden behind a rolling partition, fellow ShadowDance Club member Bryant Davis had helped engineer the excavation and reinforcement of the alternate entrance as an emergency escape route.

Mitch Grayson had designed state-of-the-art electronics for the doors and two floor-to-ceiling steel gates that were now hidden deep inside the tunnel. The other end of the tunnel opened onto the Lamonts' land on the other side of the river. That entrance had already been secured by a reinforced steel gate just inside a large cave, so he'd coordinated with Alex and Zach to make it a secure escape route from both ends.

They'd known many of their friends and family members felt they were a bunch of paranoid bastards, but since their loved ones didn't understand the type of people they'd been dealing with for years, they didn't understand how completely reasonable the measures they'd taken were. The old mill had been built during World War II and had doubled as a bomb shelter for the people of the entire valley, so the whole structure was a virtual fortress.

Noah had installed a modern elevator, but he still liked using the open freight elevator, part of the old building's charm. But it was the floating helix staircase he'd designed himself that was one of his favorite features. Five-foot-wide slabs of granite were suspended by thick cables, so the entire thing almost appeared to be floating in mid-air.

The bottom floor was used for storage and parking, but the casual observer wouldn't ever suspect it even existed. Entering from the street, casual observers wouldn't notice the enormous open gallery and office areas actually made up the second floor of the building. When guests entered the front doors, the curving black stairway was the first thing that caught their eye—that distraction had been a deliberate piece of the interior design.

The third floor had been used to build numerous rooms with various settings he'd be able to use for private photo sessions. He didn't need the income anymore since his years working as a photojournalist and fashion photographer had paid him very well. He'd also invested his inheritance wisely in addition to his very lucrative sideline as a contractor for various governments which had been extremely profitable. Now photography could be his passion rather than a career, and he planned to enjoy creating art again after all his years of putting what he loved on the back burner.

Just thinking about taking Ilaina's picture in a couple of the sets he'd created was enough to send his blood rushing south. He couldn't wait to make love to her, then capture her sated spirit on film. Those pictures would always be for his own enjoyment—that side of his *Cara* wasn't for anyone else to see. The only picture he'd ever taken of her had been locked in a vault for years because he'd been unwilling to share it with the world.

The damned thing was worth a fortune now that she was an international fashion and modeling icon, but it would never be for sale. He was apprehensive about showing it to her because it showed the vulnerability that was at her core, but he also wanted her to see herself as he'd remembered her all these years.

She'd been quiet on the drive over to the warehouse. He watched her eyes widen as the hidden door along the river side of the building slid open, and he drove inside. She surprised him when she giggled, then looked at him shyly.

"I'm sorry, I wasn't laughing at you. I was laughing because I'm pretty sure that kind of technology wasn't available when this building was closed down, and it sure wasn't around when it was built. So, I'm assuming there are a lot more surprises yet to come, am I right?"

"Yes, you are. I'm impressed you made that observation so quickly. I've worked with the Lamonts, Bryant Davis, and Mitch Grayson on the security of this building. This is one of the safest places around, I can promise you that, *Cara*. I'll make sure you have a key fob, so you can always come in if you need a safe haven."

He saw her curious look and appreciated that she didn't ask him to explain. There would be plenty of time for all of that later, but right now, he felt like a kid with a new toy he couldn't wait to show off to the prettiest girl in the class.

"I usually take the freight elevator, but if you feel uncomfortable with it, we can use the new one." He saw a glint of mischief in her eyes as she scanned the area.

"The freight elevator sounds like fun. Lead the way... you have piqued my curiosity now. I'm anxious to see what you have created."

Smiling at the hint of challenge in her words, he helped her from the truck, then placed his hand on her lower back as he led her to the large elevator. He enjoyed the feel of the soft curve just above her ass and the gentle rocking motion of her hips as she walked confidently beside him. When he raised the metal gate, he saw her eyes widen when she saw how large the elevator was.

'Wow, you could get a car in here. This is amazing. I'll bet this was a big help with your renovations." He laughed because the old elevator had been one of the last things he'd managed to get restored.

"Actually, not so much since it's only been functional for the past few weeks. It turned out to be incredibly difficult to find parts for the blasted thing. I had to get a small company in New Mexico to make the pieces we needed, and while their work was flawless, it wasn't exactly speedy." She smiled, and he was pleased to see she seemed perfectly at ease.

"How long did it take you to complete this project?" He laughed out loud because he would probably always consider the building to be a work in progress.

"Well, as you'll soon see, it isn't exactly finished yet. I sometimes get called out—often at a moment's notice, as you well know. But now that I'm planning to retire from all that, I hope I can finish up the last few loose ends and start taking pictures again."

They had finally reached the ground floor, and he watched her take in her surroundings as he raised the metal gate. When they stepped off the elevator, her eyes widened when she saw the pictures he'd taken of children all over the world. He'd hoped for that exact reaction because so much of what he had to tell her involved kids.

She already knew his last call had involved a child, and he could hardly wait to get his most recent pictures of Myla uploaded so they could be printed. Placing his hand on her back again, he gently steered her toward the wall of pictures where he'd hung all but the very latest shots of the little, dark-eyed beauty who had stolen his and so many of his friends' hearts. He knew the minute she saw his little doll by the way her eyes went impossibly wide with the same wonder he felt every time he looked at her.

"Who is she? She is absolutely exquisite." Ilaina's voice was a reverent whisper. Noah didn't answer for several seconds because he was fascinated watching Ilaina's eyes as she perused the photos like the professional she was. "Her beauty radiates from deep in her soul. Her heart has bled, but her soul sings."

As does yours, my sweet Cara.

"Have you heard Cash mention a child a member of his SEAL team fathered? A young girl the rest of the team has sort of adopted after her father was killed?" When she nodded without ever moving her eyes from Myla's photos, he continued. "Well, Ilaina Red Cloud meet Myla Smith." When she turned to him with wide eyes, he smiled and shook his head.

"Before you ask—no, that is not her real surname. I'll explain more about that later. This little beauty steals the heart of everyone she comes into contact with. She is the reason Alex called me away from our date, *Cara*. The nuns who have been caring for her needed my help. I'm not certain she is safe yet, but until Alex clears a few more hurdles to get her to the United States, all we can do is send up our prayers."

"What sort of danger is she in? She is just a child. Who would want to hurt her? Isn't she a United States citizen?" Noah watched as Ilaina's eyes went from soft and appreciative to dancing with a defensive fire for a child she didn't even know. *Definitely my kind of woman.*

"It's a long story, but basically, Myla was *safe* with her mother's family as long as her father was sending cash for her care. After he died, the mother's family decided to sell the girl into marriage, which is a common practice in that part of the world. Unfortunately, Alex and the rest of the team found out too late to stop the money from changing hands. Now the 'future husband' wants Myla delivered to his home. He is a powerful man and is making a lot of trouble. We are trying to negotiate with his representatives which is a polite way of saying we're trying to pay him off so we can get her out of the country. Yes, technically she is a U.S. citizen, but as I'm sure you are aware, that doesn't mean anything in some parts of the world."

This conversation was getting more involved than he'd intended, and he wanted to move her along before she got so bogged down in this problem, she forgot they were here to spend time together. He had other things he wanted to show her. He gently moved her forward and smiled when she looked back over her shoulder at Myla's pictures.

"Promise me you'll show me her updated pictures and keep me posted on her." She blushed and added, "I know if you just returned from there, you have pictures in that camera you carry everywhere that are more current, and I can't wait to see them. There is just something about her that calls to me. I can't explain it."

"I promise.' Turning, so they were facing one another, he gently threaded his fingers through her hair and cupped her cheek in his palm. *"Cara,* I want you to know, I'm deeply touched by your interest in Myla. She is a joy, and we'll talk more about her later. Right now, I have other things I want to show you.

Chapter 4

"PEOPLE DON'T SURPRISE me very often, Noah, but I have to say, you are turning out to be one surprise after another."

Noah was taken aback by her words and knew his quick inhalation probably gave him away. Standing back, watching as she strolled contentedly through his gallery, it had been easy to tell she was genuinely surprised at the quality of his work and at the breadth of the subject matter. Most people only knew him as a fashion photographer, they knew very little about what all he'd done professionally. He was completely gobsmacked when she turned to him and inquired.

"Why didn't we ever work together? Why did you purposefully avoid working with me? I know you turned down some very lucrative offers that would have put us together. What I've never understood was… why?" She must have read his stunned expression because she added, "I'm sorry if I surprised you. I guess I've gotten to be a lot more direct as I've gotten older. I've found it saves a lot of time if you know what I mean. I always assumed you left that night because you had gotten what you wanted and preferred to avoid the awkward morning after talk. But earlier, you mentioned you were called away, then tonight, Alex said there might be another reason you have acted as if I've had the plague all these years."

*Is she fucking serious? Of course, I've avoided her. If my en-
emies—and they were many—knew how much I care about her,
there wouldn't have been a safe place on Earth for her.*

He knew he was taking too long to answer, but honestly, he was working hard to pull the words together without
sounding like a paranoid bastard. It was going to be a fine
line to walk, and he knew it. On the one hand, if he didn't
tell her the truth straight up, she'd know he was lying, and
if he told her everything, she'd think he was either a nut-
case or just trying to make excuses.

"*Cara*, there is so much I want to tell you, and I will in
good time. Suffice to say, I didn't work with you because I
knew I could not have done it without everyone knowing
exactly how I feel about you. I've made some powerful
enemies during my years of traveling, and I didn't want
them to know how important you were to me." He took a
deep breath, then met her coal-black eyes once again. "I
don't know exactly what Alex told you, but I'm betting it's
something along that order because it's the simple truth,
and I've never known Alex Lamont to lie."

Noah watched as her face flushed a pale rose color.
He'd always marveled at the amazing light caramel color of
her skin and how her blush was still so easy to see. Ilaina's
Native American fathers had given her all the very best
features of their heritage, and she'd gotten the best of her
mother's Anglo features as well. The combination had
been heart-stopping from the time she had been a very
young girl. Noah understood why her oldest brother Cash
had been an over-protective bastard, but it hadn't made
him hate it any less.

"Okay, I'll let it go for now because I'd really like to see
more of your work. I'm also curious to see what all you

have done with this building. So far, the whole place has been a wonderful surprise. The modern interior is a stark contrast to the old brick serviceability of the exterior, and the functionality of the design is amazing. This is exactly the sort of place I'd have chosen for myself."

Her smile lit up the room, and he was grateful she moved on through the gallery. That it was the kind of place she would have chosen for herself pleased him more than she could imagine. There would be plenty of space to share, but he kept that tidbit to himself. He'd hung her picture in his office and was saving that stop for last. When they'd reached the closed door that led to his office, he turned her, so she was facing him. Reaching up he used his fingers to lift her chin so he could look into her eyes.

"*Cara*, this is my office, and there is a very special picture hanging inside. It seems as though I've waited forever to show it to you." He pressed his lips to her forehead. Lingering there while he enjoyed the warmth of her skin and the tantalizing scent of citrus and sage, Noah wanted to make a memory of this moment. When he finally pulled back, he met her gaze and smiled.

"I want you to see the woman I loved enough to stay away from but held tight to the memory of the moment in time when this picture was taken."

He quickly opened the door because he could see the clouds move through her eyes, and he damned well didn't want to give the storm a chance to break. When he stepped aside, he saw her eyes go straight to the picture hanging over the mantle of the native stone fireplace that dominated the wall facing them. All he could do was stand back and watch as she slowly advanced until she was standing directly in front of the most meaningful picture he'd ever taken. He didn't say anything, he just waited.

ILAINA HAD HEARD Noah's words, and for a second, she had thought he was going to show her a picture of another woman, but then he'd thrown open the door, and she'd been too stunned to speak. Looking at the image, she'd been completely bowled over. Between one heartbeat and the next, she knew exactly when the shot had been taken, and realizing he'd truly captured exactly how she'd been feeling at that moment was as thrilling as it was humbling. For long seconds, she just looked at the picture, seeing for the first time the vulnerable young woman she had been at that moment. It was sad to realize she'd become someone entirely different in the years since. She was much more jaded, and she wasn't sure she liked the person she had become.

"Noah... I don't know what to say. I really don't. I've had hundreds of thousands of pictures taken since this one, but none I liked as much." She heard his breath release in a huff and wondered if he had even realized he'd been holding it. No doubt he'd feared her reaction, but he shouldn't have. She felt her eyes fill with tears because she remembered the words he'd spoken in the hall, and then it occurred to her that he'd kept the painting for himself. She didn't doubt he'd know its value, yet he'd never shared it with anyone.

"Where has this been?" He smiled at her, and she noticed the wistful look in his eyes.

"I kept it wrapped and in a vault. Alex and Zach knew if anything ever happened to me, it was to go to you or your family. It was never intended for public display despite the fact it is the most beautiful, sensual picture I've ever taken. The truth is I just didn't want to share this intimate side of you with anyone else."

She hadn't even realized tears heavy with emotions were rolling down her cheeks until he leaned over and kissed them away.

"This picture was the only tangible thing I had to hold on to from that night. I can still look at this picture and feel the dewy velvet of your skin as it brushed against mine. I remember exactly how your sweet honey imprinted itself as the most erotic perfume I'd ever smelled and the look of wonder in your eyes as I slid into your heat for the first time. Everything about that night was pure magic. The windows welcomed the moonlight, inviting it to caress your nipples until they were perfect beaded treasures. The shadows created by the moon dancing with the clouds as it worshipped you only served to add to the allure and mystery of the night.

"I have looked at the smaller copy of this picture a million times so I could let my mind drift back to that night. This picture allowed me to freeze frame that moment in time. There have been many nights when I'd look at it just before falling asleep, so you were the last thing I saw before I closed my eyes. It let me dream of you in colors I don't think have even been named yet."

Ilaina let her own memories drift over her and closed her eyes as she became more and more lost in his words. When he stopped speaking, she slowly opened her eyes.

"I'm glad you showed it to me… for many reasons, but most of all I'm grateful because it allows me an opportunity to see how you saw me that night. That insight is one of the most meaningful and sincere compliments I've ever received. It also highlights how much I long to be able to trust someone as much as the woman in the picture trusts the man holding the camera. In that picture, I see a young woman who trusted and loved with her whole heart... I lost that somewhere along the way, but I'd like very much to find my way back there again."

She hadn't realized how much she missed the woman she had been until confronted with her image. When had she become so jaded? Had it started that night and continued to unfurl like a rose in full bloom? It was an apt analogy because even though she knew she was beautiful on the outside, Lainy also knew she wasn't as pretty on the inside... the thorns surrounding her heart were all too real.

She finally realized she had been lost in thought for several long seconds, and Noah was waiting quietly and looking at her thoughtfully. He waited for her to *come back* and focus once again on their conversation before he started speaking to her in a soothing voice.

"*Cara*, that woman is still very much alive and well, she is just waiting to be set free once again. Come." He took her small hand in his much larger, calloused one and led her from his office and up the most incredible stairway she'd ever seen.

Wide slabs of gleaming black granite—polished smooth on the top but left rough-cut on the bottoms and sides—were suspended by cables, so the entire staircase gave the impression it was suspended in the air. Its gentle spiral design accented the stonework and the open feeling of the entire structure. She wanted to ask him about it but didn't want to break the sudden sexual tension she felt between them. If she dared to be honest with herself, she knew how much her soul ached with a deep need to feel that connection again.

Noah kept her hand clasped in his as they walked down

the hallway, and she smiled at the pictures hanging on the walls. These were the type of pictures you might find in anyone's home—shots of his family and friends. Lainy knew he'd lost both of his parents a couple of years earlier. His mom had died after a short but intense battle with breast cancer, and his father had died of a heart attack only a few months later. She remembered her mom telling her everyone who knew them swore the elder Drummond had surely died of a broken heart.

Lainy hadn't known his parents well, but she recognized them easily in the photos. There were pictures of the three of them taken all over the world. His father had been a very wealthy entrepreneur, and she had always figured those trips had been the catalyst for Noah becoming an international sensation as a photographer. When she pulled him to a stop so she could look at the pictures, he smiled and nodded. She traced over the edges of several of the frames showing his family at the Eiffel Tower and The Great Wall of China.

"Did you become a photographer so you could continue traveling the world?"

He was leaning against a door frame, smiling when she finally looked up at him, waiting for his answer. His smile had always been devastating, and she always thought he belonged in front of the camera as much as behind it.

"Yes and no. My parents always made sure I saw both sides of the cities we visited. We may have seen all the beautiful landmarks, but they also made certain I understood there was a whole other side as well. They wanted me to know there was a lot of poverty and pain tucked behind of those beautiful structures." He paused for several seconds, and she could see him debating with himself about how much he should reveal. "I wanted to be able to document the starkness of those inequities—make certain the world didn't forget those who were so easily overlooked. Very quickly, I discovered I was in a unique position to help in some rather significant ways."

Lainy knew when he decided the conversation had veered too far off-track… the shutdown reflected equally in his eyes and the sudden stiffness in his posture. Grasping her hand, he lifted it slowly and pressed a soft kiss against her knuckles.

"But right now, my sweet, I have other plans for you."

She watched as he stepped forward and when he used the fingers of his free hand to trace her bottom lip, she felt her breath catch and moisture flood her pussy.

"*Cara*, I am going to tell you exactly what I want. *I want you.* I want to feel your bare skin against mine as I map every inch of you with my lips. I ache to watch the chill bumps of arousal race over your smooth, tanned skin. I want to feel how your body responds to mine as I slide my throbbing cock inside your pulsing heat. I want to hold you in my arms as you come apart when we both find the release we are craving."

Oh boy. He certainly hadn't been kidding about telling her exactly what he wanted. He painted a pretty amazing picture in her mind—she could hardly wait to feel his velvet covered steel pushing inside her. There was a small part of her brain that considered she might be giving in too easily, but just the glimmer of that thought brought a riot of protests from her other body parts. She opened her mouth and tried to find her voice so she could reply, but it had deserted her. Finally, she just slowly closed her mouth once again and nodded. He laced his fingers with hers and raised her hand again, but this time, he turned it so that he could kiss her palm.

"Come on, sweetheart, let me love you." His voice was soft, and his words sounded like a simple benediction. At that moment, Lainy knew her heart was in big trouble once again.

SITTING IN HIS rental car, reviewing the pictures he'd taken of Ilaina inside while she had been dancing with the other women, Maxwell Bradford wondered how surprised she was going to be when he started sharing them with her over the next few weeks. Thinking back on the evening he met the infamous Ilaina, he was still torn between who he should be the angriest at—her or himself.

Granted, he'd had too much to drink and shouldn't have tried to initiate a conversation with her, but she hadn't been unhappy with his company until he'd tried to kiss her. They'd been getting along great until that moment, then she'd suddenly turned into an ice princess. Hell, he'd sent flowers the next day, along with a note of apology and offered to take her to a great place for dinner, but she hadn't even bothered to return his call. By the time he'd gotten back to the hotel after his presentation, she'd already checked out.

It hadn't taken him long to find Ilaina again, after all, finding lost people was a large part of his business. He'd been tracking her for months, and her steadfast refusal to re-engage with him was really beginning to annoy him. He didn't want to hurt her, he just wanted her.

He'd finally decided if it took scaring her a bit to get her in his bed, that was what he'd do. Once he finally managed to corner her here in her hometown, he found out she was going to be in that big house all alone for the next several weeks. He'd gotten some great shots tonight he planned to send her while her brothers and new sister-in-law were on their honeymoon. After he laid that groundwork, he'd angle an introduction through their mutual friends and play the white knight, riding in to save her from a dangerous stalker.

His plan had been coming together nicely until some other man had suddenly entered the picture. Max had watched as the man—one of the waitresses helpfully identified as Noah Drummond—wrapped his arms around Ilaina as if he had every right to, then practically seduced her on the dance floor, in full view of her family and friends.

Christ, she has a conniption fit when I try to kiss her, this guy comes in from nowhere, and she melts into his arms? Who the fuck is Noah Drummond, and why did my woman leave with him?

It was time to get the hell out of Dodge before he attracted any unwanted attention. He'd gotten his pictures and also managed a *chance* meeting with Alex Lamont. Max had greeted one of the men he knew called the shots for Lamont Holdings and had given him a business card, after all, they were in businesses that would work well together. One of the things Max did best was laying his groundwork in meticulous detail. Better the Lamonts' security team was working with him than against him.

As he pulled out on to the highway leading out of the small mountain town, Max couldn't help smiling about how close he'd been to his sweet angel again. She walked right by him on her way down the narrow hallway leading to the ladies' room. Her beautiful hair had brushed over his arm in a silky wave when she'd turned suddenly to answer a friend's call. He nearly came from the smell of her perfume alone.

He never had trouble getting women into his bed, so why was he so obsessed with Ilaina? Was it because she had run? Or that every straight man on the planet had seen her face and lusted for her? Or was there really something *that* special about the woman? Max honestly didn't know and feared the answer was some mixture of all of those reasons. The one thing he did know was his game would need to be stepped up now that Noah Drummond had entered the picture. Max wouldn't tip his hand just yet, but soon—*very soon*, she would be his.

Chapter 5

N OAH SHOULD HAVE been exhausted. He had traveled straight through for so many hours the time zones had started to blur together. He'd been determined to get back in time for the Red Clouds' wedding and hated that he'd missed the actual ceremony. Alex had been keeping him posted and had smoothed his trip back at every stop. It had been a frustrating and exhausting trip, but the minute he'd seen Ilaina dancing, his fatigue had evaporated like a summer rain on the sun-baked earth of the hell-hole he'd left almost forty hours ago.

Seeing her eyes go wide as he led her into the master suite's spa bath made every cent of his guilty indulgence money well spent. The black and gray color scheme had been a nod to his love of the shadows and highlights created in black and white erotic photos. He couldn't wait to get back into the studio and start creating once again.

Alex and Zach had already asked him to spend time photographing their wife Katarina, and they'd actually had some great ideas for intimate shots they wanted taken. Their only request was that one of them was present during her sessions. He'd agreed and laughed when they'd told him they had attended every doctor's appointment with her until Bree Hart had joined the staff at the local hospital. Alex had chuckled and said every Dom at The

ShadowDance Club had breathed a sigh of relief when Bree married Jamie Creed and Ethan Jantz and decided to make Climax her new home.

Dimming the lights, Noah let his hands speak for him as he silently stripped her of her clothes before quickly removing his own. Starting the water in the shower, he made all the necessary adjustments, then led her inside. Standing under the rain soaking shower heads, moving his soap covered hands over Ilaina's toned body was the very definition of a sensual experience. If he closed his eyes, it was easy to imagine the two of them standing beneath a waterfall hidden deep in the jungle, alone but surrounded by so many living things.

He had already shampooed her beautiful hair and knew his Bulgari Aqua shower gel was going to smell a lot better on her than it did on him. She leaned forward and brushed her peaked nipples against his chest.

"Now I know why you always smell like a warm ocean breeze racing over a field of freshly cut grass and sage. Every time I caught a whiff of this scent, I looked for you. I followed a man for two blocks one evening in Buenos Aires just so I could lose myself in the memories of this scent."

When Noah looked down at her, he noticed she'd closed her eyes, but he wasn't going to let her hide her passion from him, so he quietly commanded, "Open your eyes, *Cara*." When she did, he smiled.

"Sweetheart, you never have to hide your emotions from me. I want to know exactly where your heart is every moment. I've lost too much time with you, and I refuse to miss another second." Noah knew he could fall into her dark eyes without a second thought, but he was determined to see through his plan for tonight. A momentary distraction would never be enough.

He quickly scrubbed the travel grime off himself before handing her one of the large, thick towels he'd laid aside. While she dried her long hair, he went into the bedroom to turn down the bed and light enough candles to bathe the entire room in a soft golden glow. Remembering she had always loved piano music, he'd started the stereo and made sure the tracks he'd chosen for her were playing by the time she walked tentatively into the room. Moving to stand in front of her, he let his fingers draw an invisible line down the side of her face, giving her a moment to settle. He could see the pulse at the base of her neck speed up, and while he wanted her excited, he sought her arousal, not her nervousness.

"*Cara*, I've been waiting for this moment for so very long. I know you may not fully understand why I kept my distance, but you must believe me—it was never because I didn't want you." He felt his cock pressing against the towel he'd wrapped around his waist and let his fingers slide down to where she'd tucked in the corner of the bath sheet she'd wrapped around herself.

"Before we get you out of this wet towel and into bed, I want to remind you I'm still a Dominant. It's a part of who I am, and while I can do sweet and tender, it won't always be like that. The one thing you can always trust is I'll have your best interests at heart. I will take that responsibility to you seriously. You have grown up with strong male role models, and I'll do my best to live up to the high standards they have set."

He knew he was probably saying more than was needed—after all, she hadn't agreed to anything beyond this moment, but he wanted her to know how committed he was to make this work. Noah didn't want to scare her off, but his father's words echoed through his mind. His dad had always said, "Begin as you intend to go—in all things."

Most people hadn't realized his mother was much more than just a wife, she'd also been his father's slave. Theirs had been a committed 24/7 total power exchange, and while Noah had never desired that type of relationship, he also understood the importance of laying out at least some of his expectations from the beginning.

He hadn't taken his eyes off her face even after he'd finished speaking and was starting to worry just before he saw a flash of relief move through her dark eyes.

"You're right, I was raised in an environment where the men dominated, but they always did it with love. My mom and I were protected... sometimes more than we wanted to be, but I always knew I was loved, and that sort of confidence is a pretty great gift."

He could tell by her eyes she wasn't finished speaking, so he waited while she put her thoughts in order.

"I have a basic understanding of the lifestyle my family lives, but I don't have any practical knowledge... well, aside from the one time you took me to The ShadowDance Club, and I think we both know that didn't end all that well."

He'd taken a young woman who hadn't been ready for the experience into a BDSM club, and she'd seen a lot of things that had frightened her. He'd never forgotten how traumatized Ilaina had been that night, and the terror he'd seen in her eyes had haunted him for years.

He was the first to admit he'd made a lot of mistakes and missteps in his life, but there were none he regretted more than those he'd made with Ilaina Red Cloud. It wasn't that he hadn't been warned. Christ, Alex and Zach Lamont had tried a thousand times warn him against making the same mistake they'd made with Katarina, but

Noah had been young and so sure he was doing the right thing. Then to top off several other mistakes, he'd done the wrong thing for all the right reasons—and the result had been disastrous. All he could do now was try to rebuild their relationship from the ashes of what he'd burned and prove he was worthy of the trust he'd failed to treasure so long ago. Giving himself an internal shake, he needed to remember looking back wasn't going to get him anywhere.

"That's good enough for now." He nodded once and smiled. "We'll work it out, I promise." He brushed his lips softly over hers before speaking close to her ear. "We'll have plenty of time to work it out, but tonight isn't about that, *Cara*. Tonight is about me making love to the woman who captured my heart and soul a very long time ago."

After he unwrapped her from the towel like the exquisite gift she was, he leaned down and scooped her up into his arms and gently laid her in the middle of his large bed. When he climbed in alongside her, he reached for her and wanted to sigh in contentment when she pressed her body against his. He felt her relax into his embrace, and he wasn't sure anything in his entire life had ever felt as perfect as this moment.

"*Cara*, you fit against me so perfectly—it's as if the angels made us for each other." He shifted, putting his knee in the perfect position to push her thighs apart, slowly increasing the pressure until his leg met the damp fold of her sex. Pushing forward in small increments, he smiled to himself when the pressure on her waxed pussy caused her to gasp slightly. Noah was confident he could bring her pleasure the likes of which she'd never known if he could gain her trust and her submission. Those things would take time, but he planned to start earning them both right now.

"The candlelight loves you, sweetness. It skims over

your skin like a stone on a calm pond. I remember how moonbeams always seemed to seek you out when we'd lay under the stars, talking for hours. We'd be on the hood of my car, side by side, yet the moon knew you were the canvas it wanted to paint in a palette of colors I'm sure were yours alone."

He continued kissing the sensitive spot behind her ear all the time he'd been speaking, relishing the subtle shudder he felt move through her body as he moved lower. He pressed his hand against the sensitive spot at the small of her back, so she arched into the kisses he rained over her collarbone and chest as he made his way to her perfect breasts.

Noah licked a slow circle around the nipple closest to him, then blew a soft puff of air over it and smiled as it responded immediately, and she moaned softly.

"I'll give you everything your body seeks, just relax and let me enjoy the gift of you. Your body is so responsive, and I am enjoying watching the way your skin flushes a deep rose as you become aroused." When he pulled her tight nipple into his mouth and pressed it against the ridges along the roof of his mouth, she started to tremble, making him wonder if he'd be able to get her off just by talking to her and playing with her luscious breasts.

"Oh God, it feels so good. It has been so long." Ilaina's words were so quiet, for a few seconds, Noah doubted she realized she had spoken them out loud. He wondered exactly how long it had been since she'd had sex—she was already closing in fast on her first release, and he'd only just started playing with her. When he started slowly trailing his fingers through her wet fold, he heard her breaths coming in short pants before she started trembling again. When he lightened his touch, she nearly growled,

"No…please don't stop. Oh, crapping crickets, I was so close." Watching Ilaina squirm, trying to get closer to his touch had to be one of the most erotic things he'd ever seen.

"Tell me what you want, sweetness. I want to hear the words." He remembered this had been a major sticking point for her before and wanted to make sure she was able to get past the obstacle now. Hell, there wasn't much of anything in the world that was a bigger turn on than a woman who could articulate her needs and desires.

"Oh… Noah, you are torturing me. You know I… I can barely think when you are just near me, and my mind shatters when you are touching me. Please let me come. Drat, I was so close."

The fact she couldn't think when he was close was certainly news to him. *Well, at least she is as affected by me as I am by her.*

He didn't respond—he learned a long time ago you often found out a lot more information if you just waited patiently. Most people tend to want to fill the silence, particularly when they are nervous. Letting his fingers feather over her clit, Noah smiled when her entire body arched off the bed. The small bundle of nerves was already fully emerged from beneath its hood in a bid for his attention, and he intended to oblige.

Ilaina had an innate, sensual beauty that seemed to draw people to her. There was a mystical quality surrounding her that defied any accurate description. He'd read a lot of the words various writers had used and often laughed when even the most seasoned writers for various media outlets admitted they didn't know exactly how to describe the unique beauty of the woman they knew only as *Ilaina*.

When he finally slid his fingers inside her, he was

stunned at the tightness he found and wondered again just how long it had been since she had had sex.

"How long, *Cara*? How long has it been since you have enjoyed this type of pleasure? How long since you've had a man's touch?" If he thought he was surprised by the tightness, he was absolutely floored by her answer. Her control was nearly gone, the words little more than panted whispers.

"There has been no one since you."

Noah felt like the world had dropped out from under him. How could a woman as sexual as Ilaina Red Cloud appeared manage to avoid the pleasures of sex for so long? Years she'd denied herself the very thing she craved. Christ, what kind of idiot men had she been around that none had wanted her as badly as he did at this moment?

Suddenly, he realized she'd faced the same challenge he had—she craved more than the sexual release itself, her heart needed the intimacy that could only be found between them. Feeling her stiffen in response to his silence, he leaned down and placed a kiss right over her navel.

"You are the most amazing woman I've ever known. Now, let's see about getting your sweet body a bit more relaxed before I slide into your wet heat. Put your hands above your head and don't move them." As soon as she had complied, he pushed two fingers into her and curved them up, easily finding his spongy target. Pressing down with both fingers, he made sure his next words were more command than entreaty.

"Come for me, my sweet *Cara*."

Chapter 6

NOAH'S WORDS HAD barely crossed his lips when Ilaina seemed to shatter right before his eyes. It was without question the most spectacular thing he had ever seen. Feeling her channel clamp down around his fingers, squeezing them with such strength made him wonder how exquisitely painful it was going to be when those pulsing vaginal walls surrounded his already aching cock. The flood of her honey over his fingers ignited a hunger to taste her that was almost more than he was able to resist, but he moved up her delectable body, so the warm breath of his words would caress her ear.

"You are even more exquisite when you come, *Cara*. Watching as your entire body flushes with the sweet glow of release is amazing. Seeing you arch into my touch brings me far more satisfaction than you could possibly know and hearing I am the only one who will ever have the privilege of witnessing that beauty is the answer to each and every prayer I've sent up to heaven since the last time I made love to you."

While she'd been catching her breath, he managed to sheath his rigid cock and was holding himself over her, resting his weight on his forearms while he stroked the sides of her face with his fingers. When she finally opened her eyes, the look of vulnerability in her gaze tugged at his heart.

"I want you with a hunger I can't begin to explain. Keep your eyes on mine, *Cara*. I want to be able to look at you when I push myself between the slick petals of your labia and sink myself in your hot pussy—your heat and wet silk wrapped around me so tightly, I can barely breathe. The smell of your arousal is like a wisp of magic tethering us together and pulling me deeper into your soul." Sliding his cock into Ilaina was the sweetest feeling in the entire world. If he died in the next minute, he knew he would go out happy.

"Fuck me, the feeling of your body wrapping itself around me is pure rapture. Your muscles are trembling in random pulses, and it is stretching my control to the point I'm afraid I'm going to just fuck you right into the mattress, love."

Noah had frozen and was mentally reviewing every boring statistic he'd ever learned, in hopes of staving off the loss of control literally beginning to blur his vision. Just as he thought he might be getting himself under control, Ilaina tilted her hips back and tightened her pelvic muscles. A bolt of lightning went from his brain directly to his balls, searing him from the inside out, but it was her softly moaned plea that detonated every bit of his restraint.

"Oh fuck, *Cara*, hang on baby, this is going to be fast and furious." He pulled her hands over her head, cuffing both wrists tightly in his hand as he set a fast pace of long strokes in and out of her soaking pussy.

"Come with me, baby." He heard her scream his name just as the electricity circulating in his balls spiked through his entire system before returning to shoot his seed out in an explosive release. Feeling the hot jets pulsing against the tip of the condom made him long for a time when they no longer had latex between them. Sealing his lips over hers, Noah felt as if she had just pulled a piece of soul from the deepest part of him and taken it into herself.

Noah knew he was tempting fate by keeping himself seated in Ilaina's sweet heat, but he couldn't help stealing just a bit more of the heaven he'd found with her vaginal walls rippling around him. Rolling to the side and taking her with him, Noah held her tightly against his chest until they'd both gotten their breathing under control.

"*Cara*, there are just no words to describe what we just shared, but I do promise round two will last longer."

"Well, I'm not sure I'll survive *longer*. Wow." Even though her words were softly spoken, he could hear the unease in her voice.

Noah quickly excused himself but returned quickly after taking care of the condom. Using a warm rag, he cleaned her sensitive tissues despite her protests and patted her dry before returning to the bed. Settling himself against her, he pulled her into his arms and smiled when he felt her relax.

"Sleep, baby, I've got you." *Know that your heart will always be safe with me. I handled things all wrong once, but I'll not make that mistake again.*

Kissing the top of her head, he tunneled his fingers under the silky curtain of her hair and gently massaged the base of her skull until he felt her breathing even out. Once he knew she was asleep, he finally allowed his eyes to close as he breathed her in.

WHEN LAINY WOKE up, it only took her a few seconds to

realize two things. First, she was surrounded by a very naked Noah Drummond, and second, she really needed to use the restroom. It took her several minutes to untangle herself from his hold without waking him, so by the time she'd finally made it to the restroom, she was fully awake. Deciding she was thirsty, she grabbed his shirt from the floor and went in search of the kitchen. She made her way down the hall, her bare feet not making a sound until she finally found what she was looking for.

The floor to ceiling windows let in enough moonlight, it was easy to find her way around the unfamiliar space. Moving back down the hall, she glanced through a doorway she hadn't noticed earlier and was surprised to find a large room that looked like it was being set up to use as an elaborate photo set. The thing that caught her eye was the baby grand piano, centered against a wall of tall windows. The beautiful instrument was centered in the moonlight as if tonight's full moon was spotlighting it, hoping to capture her attention. She knew Noah had never played the piano, but he knew she did. Losing herself in music had always been a way for her to escape various kinds of stress or the full reality of any daily pressure she might have been feeling.

Moving closer so she could run her fingers over the smooth finish of the gleaming instrument, she felt the warmth of its musical potential almost as if it was a living thing. Sitting down on the bench seat, she felt an almost magnetic draw as her fingers found the gleaming ivory keys. She had always longed to have a piano exactly like this one.

Ilaina remembered the night she and Noah talked about it. They'd been leaning back against a bench in the city park, watching as a movie was shown on a giant screen during the summer festival before their senior year. It had been an old Ginger Rogers and Gene Kelly movie, and she'd commented on the beautiful piano the two were dancing on.

After she sighed and admitted how much she would love to have one like it, Noah had taken her hand in his, pulled it to his lips, and kissed the back of her hand.

"*Cara*, someday I will buy you one that is even better." She wondered if it was possible he'd remembered that long ago promise when he'd bought this beauty.

When she softly depressed one of the keys and heard the clear tone resonate through the room, she was lost. Before she even realized what she was doing, her fingers were dancing over the keys, making love to them in a way only a person who truly loved music could understand. It was easy to lose yourself in the wonder of good melodies, especially when the instrument was designed for musical perfection.

Ilaina had always believed music was meant to heal and comfort the human spirit. Many pieces were reflections of the composer's state of mind, the ebb and flow of emotion evident in the composition of the song itself. When she played, she was able to forget everything but the music—it had always been a sweet refuge for her soul.

One time, she'd let a crew she was working with know she could play, and they badgered her to play in the hotel bar. It had been the only time she'd ever played and not enjoyed the experience, so she'd never again mentioned her musical skill to anyone else.

She didn't give any thought to where she was or how little she was wearing, she just played. The music picked her up and swept her out to sea on a wave—she relished the feeling of just being along for the ride. Lainy didn't know how long she had been playing—completely immersed in the depth of the emotional release—but she suddenly became aware of someone standing behind her just a second before she felt Noah's warm hands caress her shoulders. When her fingers stilled, she felt his warm breath against her ear.

"Don't stop, *Cara*. It's yours, you know? I made you a promise one night a long time ago… and this is my way of showing you I will always honor the promises I make to you. Play for me, love."

NOAH HAD COME awake the minute Ilaina picked up his shirt and made her way out of the bedroom. Watching her pull the fabric to her nose and inhale his scent had sent a shot of pure erotic lust straight through him. It was one of the most sensual things he'd ever seen a woman do. He waited several minutes before grabbing a pair of boxers and going down the hall to find her. When he saw her in what he'd dubbed the music room, running her fingers over the piano he'd recently purchased for her, he'd been stunned at the scene unfolding in front of him. Stepping silently into the next room, he grabbed a camera he knew was set to take low light shots and silently slipped back into the room with Ilaina.

Standing back in the shadows, he took pictures as silvery moonlight filtered through the windows and waltzed over her dark hair still tousled from their lovemaking. There were simply no words to describe how beautiful she was. If he'd set up the scene, he wouldn't have been able to make it any better than this.

The sensuality of the lighting, the musical setting, and the woman herself—the entire scene was beyond description. He knew he'd save these pictures and show them to their children and grandchildren one day. He wanted their family to understand her beauty had shone from the inside, and what the public had seen was merely the lovely outer wrapping.

Watching her play was like observing someone transported to a whole new plane. The music had been hauntingly familiar and had taken him several minutes to remember it was from an old movie they'd watched on television during their senior year of high school. He couldn't remember the name of the movie, but he remembered how she had cried at the end. He'd teased her, and she'd smacked him with a pillow before dissolving into a fit of giggles.

Seeing her sitting across the room, wearing nothing but his shirt with the moon as her spotlight, lost in the music was without question the most beautiful thing he'd ever seen. He could only hope the camera had captured the essence of the moment. After he'd taken several more shots, he set the camera off to the side and walked up behind her. Encouraging her to keep playing, he simply stood behind her and let her love of the music fill him as well.

Feeling the passion Ilaina had for the music reminded him of his passion for capturing beauty on film. He knew she was planning to start a marketing business and hoped she'd be interested in helping him promote his gallery and studio. Noah had used various public relations firms in the past but had never worked with anyone who really understood his love of photography. Noah knew Katarina Lamont was talking to Ilaina about a couple of collaborations for her web design business, so perhaps he needed to work with both women.

Setting all thoughts of business aside, Noah focused on this moment, cherishing his time with his woman as she enjoyed a gift he'd given her. She'd hesitated briefly when he'd first touched her, but he was pleased when she quickly settled and returned her attention to the music as her fingers moved effortlessly over the pristine ivory keys.

He smiled as she once again let the music wash over her. Noah watched her reflection in the windows as she closed her eyes, and in a flash of insight, he saw that same the expression on her face as she rocked their child. It had been a brief glimpse into the future. He chuckled to himself because he knew, somewhere in the night, Níyol Red Cloud was smiling at her success.

Chapter 7

L AINY WAS STRETCHED out on the sun-warmed rocks surrounding the waterfall pool in the gardens behind the Lamonts' beautiful home, listening to her friends chatter about all things children and Dom related. It had been almost a week since she spent the night at Noah's, and even though they had spoken on the phone nearly every day, she hadn't actually seen him since he kissed her goodbye at her front door the next morning. He'd stayed long enough to make sure she made it inside safely, then driven away.

Sure, she'd told him she had a ton of work to do this week, and it had been the truth, but she still had worried he was deliberately putting distance between them again, and that was frustrating and disheartening. Most of her frustration was because she knew she shouldn't care—but she did.

Cripes, this is exactly why I have avoided this kind of relationship drama. It's too hard to navigate and exhausting as well. I don't have the time or energy to get my heart broken again.

"Hey, girlfriend. You gonna answer my question or just sit there staring off into space, drooling about Noah Drummond all day?" Kat's voice cut through the fog and jolted Lainy back to the moment.

"Shit. I'm sorry, I was indeed lost in thought, but I'm

not copping to it being about Noah. And just so you know, I'm withdrawing my nomination of you as Hostess of the Year for that crack. Now, what did you ask me?" Lainy smiled at Kat so her friend would know she'd been teasing, appreciating they'd all fallen into an easy rapport.

Jenna Matthews quickly muffled a bark of laughter with her hand which made the baby she was breastfeeding jerk at the sharp noise his mother had made. Jenna had been Kat's best friend forever, and since Kat's marriage to her brothers, they were now sisters-in-law as well. She and Colt Matthews had been married only a short time, but from what Lainy had heard, they had known each other for years because he'd been a Navy SEAL assigned to the same Team as Jenna's brothers, Alex and Zach.

Looking over at the tiny woman, it was hard to believe the trauma Lainy knew Jenna had endured. After being raped by a member of her brother's Team who had been welcomed into the Lamonts' home to recover from an injury, Jenna spent years hiding the assault because the man had threatened to kill one or both of her brothers.

The young woman her brothers nicknamed "The Warrior Fairy," funneled her energy into becoming a martial arts and self-defense expert. Lainy had heard several of the subs at The ShadowDance Club had recently begun pestering Jenna to start teaching self-defense classes. Lainy planned to take advantage of those if they managed to persuade the new mother to get started.

"Jesus Christ… uh, Superstar… focus already, Lainy." Kat was laughing and looking up into the trees. "Shit… crap… well fuck it, I give up. The video is probably already being live-streamed by Spies-R-Us, anyway."

Rissa balanced her small plate of fruit on her rounded belly and smiled at Lainy.

"Oh yeah, Kat is toast. This whole place is wired for sight and sound. My Mitch is a techy genius, and if you fart out here, he's gonna know what you had for lunch yesterday." Looking up into the same trees, Lainy watched Rissa smile and speak into oblivion. "See lover, I'm a much sweeter sub than Kat." She then turned to her friends, and whispered, "Well, smarter anyway. My feet ache, and I'm angling for a massage later." Within seconds Rissa's phone vibrated on the table beside her, and when she picked it up, the beautiful redhead leaned her head back and burst out laughing. "Well, it seems I'm going to get that foot massage after all... and more according to this message. So, ladies, I'd say the sight and sound systems are working just fine."

"Message received, and thanks for the warning. Now, back to Sister Silence over there." Kat waved her hand toward Lainy and continued, "What's up, sweet cheeks? Not getting enough? God knows that can send a girl into a funk."

Lainy was just staring at her with her mouth dropped open when Kat's phone started ringing. When the little blonde dynamo glanced at the screen, she swore, "Frack." When she answered using her sweetest voice, all the women burst out laughing.

"Hello, husband mine... no, I did not say I knew that from personal experience... no, I did not say that either... are you fu—I mean, seriously?" Lainy watched Kat closely as her new friend continued listening to whichever one of her husbands had called. Suddenly, Kat's face was flushed, her breathing rapid, and her eyes drifted closed.

Tori Bartell leaned over and whispered in Lainy's ear, "Watch her closely. That will be Alex on the phone, and he's going to make her come using nothing but his voice and words. He does this to her when they're dancing as well. From what I've heard, your brother Collin can do the same thing to Layla. Oh shoot, maybe that was too much information, sorry about that. I swear, I used to have better personal boundaries, but Kat really is a bad influence." They both snickered just as Kat's soft moan filled the air.

Several minutes later, Kat seemed to have caught her breath and laughed about how satisfying her "punishment" had been. Lainy found herself enjoying the company of the women, and that alone was a surprise. For years, she had been surrounded by the cut-throat competition of fashion and advertisement modeling industry, and she'd learned early on, women weren't particularly nice to one another. Hell, most of the time they were downright vicious, so Lainy had a deep appreciation for the friendships she had formed since moving back to Colorado.

Kat seemed to have refocused her attention on a young woman named Sally. From what Lainy could gather from the conversation, the woman was involved with one of the Doms at The Club and also headed up The Club's housekeeping which, from what she heard, was a monumental task.

Her friends explained Sally had taken over The Club's housekeeping unit when it had been rife with challenges, but it hadn't taken the young, single mother long to turn the department into an efficient and well-operated part of The Club. Sally's efforts had earned the respect of both Alex and Zach in the process.

Kat's grin turned almost feral as she inquired, "So, how are things with Cort?"

Lainy was about to feel sorry for Sally until she shot back, "Kat, I'm warning you... I love you like a sister, but you better keep your match-making-mitts outta our business, or I'll sing like a canary."

Lainy noticed several of the women freeze and wondered if maybe she'd let down her guard too soon when Kat turned and burst out laughing. Judging by Kat's reaction, she didn't mind being called out by Sally, and that alone was enough to further endear the women to Lainy.

Kat's snorted, "Well, damn. No need to get your panties in a twist," sent all the women, Lainy included, into howls of laughter. For the first time in years, she really felt like she *fit in*, and it was so liberating.

They discussed her brothers and their new wife's plan to return from their honeymoon the next week. Lainy knew her brothers had planned to be gone longer, but Layla was anxious to get back. After all the work she'd done for the new motel, she'd been adamant about being involved with all the preparations for the new facility's grand opening which was fast approaching.

When Lainy had talked to Layla on the phone, she hadn't been surprised to hear her new sister-in-law's comment that her brothers' different definitions of "downtime" was a challenge she was quickly tiring of dealing with.

Lainy was sure it was her middle brother Collin who was causing the most trouble. Collin was the strictest of the three Doms and was also a total tight ass, in Lainy's opinion. He was absolutely brilliant and richer than God, thanks to his wildly successful software and game development business, but his tendency to "over plan" everything wouldn't be fun on a honeymoon. Ilaina was looking forward to working with him professionally, hell, his recommendations alone would likely gain her several clients.

Personally, Lainy would be relieved when they returned because the recent emails she'd received from her stalker led her to believe he might have figured out where she was hiding. The thought of him showing up in Climax was more than a bit terrifying. She'd actually considered mentioning it to Noah, but considering the odd distance between them, she hadn't felt comfortable enough to trouble him with her problems. Maybe she should ask these ladies who they could recommend to review her home's security system. Looking around at the women chatting amiably, Lainy noticed Tori seemed to be fading quickly.

"Tori, are you ready to go? I'd be happy to give you a ride home. I'm not really comfortable having you driving when you are obviously exhausted." Lainy had known Tori's husband Trace her entire life and didn't think she'd ever known anyone nicer. He'd already lost one woman he'd loved dearly, Lainy wasn't about to risk him losing another or the sweet child Tori was carrying.

When Tori blinked her eyes in Lainy's general direction, it was obvious the sleepy woman was trying to focus on her face.

"Oh, well, yes, that would be nice, thanks so much for the offer, but I should probably call my husband and see what he has planned." All the women snickered when Tori's phone started ringing. Lainy could tell from Tori's end of the conversation. Trace was already on his way, so she smiled and waved at her sweet friend. Excusing herself, Lainy gathered her things, intending to head up to the house.

Leaning over close to Jenna, Lainy asked, "Who would you recommend to review a home's security system?" At Jenna's startled look, she quickly added, "I haven't had any trouble, well, not really, but I've been dealing with a cyber-stalker for a while now and... well, he likes to allude to the fact he knows where I live, so I'd just like to make sure my family is safe."

Jenna smiled. "I know you think you said all of that quietly enough that I was the only person who heard it, but I can assure you that's not the case. I'm also sure you'll be getting more help than you bargained for and probably in fairly short order too."

Lainy saw her phone flash with first one incoming message, then two. She'd looked up to speak to Jenna when she heard the distinctive ring-tone she'd assigned to Noah. *Good grief. And here I thought I only had one stalker.*

Picking up the phone, she answered and assured Noah she would indeed explain and forward the emails to Mitch as soon as she got home, and even though he wasn't happy, she managed to get him off the phone quickly. Shaking her head, she smiled at Jenna who just shrugged her shoulders as if to say, "I tried to warn you."

Lainy said her goodbyes and made her way toward the back of the house, taking her time, enjoying the beautifully landscaped gardens. The entire area was enclosed by the two wings of the Lamonts' mansion, and a third wing housed The ShadowDance Club. The fourth side was a beautiful stand of tall trees, providing the perfect backdrop for the lush paradise that lay at the base of the rock wall. It had always seemed as if God himself had carved out a plateau at the peak of the mountain to give the Lamonts a breathtaking view in all directions, and the gardens were proof their gratitude for the gift hadn't been ignored. The gazebo and bridge over the small rock-lined stream were among her favorite features.

She recently learned those were designed and built by Rissa's second husband, Bryant Davis who had worked in conjunction with Lamont matriarch, Catherine. Lainy had heard the entire area was absolutely breathtakingly beautiful at night due to the special effect lighting and could hardly wait to see it for herself. Hopefully, there would be a party or Club event soon because Lainy had been experiencing a bit of cabin fever and was looking forward to a night out.

Chapter 8

WALKING IN THE back door of the Lamont mansion, the first person she saw was the Lamonts' long-time housekeeper, Selita. The older Latino woman ran forward, throwing her arms around Lainy, giving her a big hug. Selita and Lainy's mother had been close friends for many years, partly because they both shared an interest in cooking. Selita had always appreciated Cora Red Cloud's fluency in several Central American dialects so Selita had been able to chatter away in Spanish without worrying the meanings of her local euphemisms would be lost in translation.

"Oh, Ilaina, I so glad to see you after your fifteen frames. You still look like an Inca princess. God's mercy, I am so happy to see you *finallys*." Lainy laughed as she remembered the other reason she loved Selita like a second mother—the woman was hell on American slang expressions, and it was always great fun to try to riddle them out.

"Selita, thank you for your warm welcome, and I'm sorry I haven't been up to see you sooner. I hoped to see you at the wedding, but I heard you were back east visiting your niece. I'm not sure I really had my full fifteen minutes of fame, and that's just fine by me. I'm awfully glad to be home." Just then, Lainy heard raised voices coming from down the hall she knew led to the Lamonts' office. Raising a brow, she looked questionably at Selita.

"Oh, that is your California waves picture cutie. He came in a few minutes ago, looking like he was on the war road. Alex is wanting to send him someplace far away to get a little girl, and he says send someone else because he doesn't want to leave you. He said you have a celery guy." The older woman gave her a nudge in the direction of the office. "You go make sure Alex doesn't make Noah's peter come out because I love my Alex, but he can wear people down some of the times, you know?"

Lainy had actually tripped when she'd heard Selita's words and had snorted back her laughter. "Selita dear, I believe that expression is 'peter out' as in getting tired or giving up... although your version does bring a much more interesting picture to mind." She and Selita giggled before Lainy moved quietly down the hall. As she approached the office, she heard Alex's quieter voice.

"We need your experience, and truthfully, Ilaina would be a real asset as well. She's traveled in that area of the world, and they love her. Take her for a location shoot and let her act as part of your smoke and mirrors."

"Are you fucking kidding me, Alex? Christ, you have asked me for some crazy shit over the years, but this takes it, man. Why would I put the woman I love in that position? Damn it, I've been telling you to hire a couple of female operatives. And I know perfectly well you've already been informed Ilaina apparently has a stalker she has conveniently failed to mention."

Lainy didn't even have to see Noah to know he was running his hands through his shaggy blond hair in frustration. Stepping into the doorway, she smiled at the men gathered there.

"Gentlemen, didn't your mamas teach you it's not nice

to leave some of the kids out of the game?" Glancing around the room, Lainy noticed several men she recognized and several more she had yet to be introduced to.

"*Cara*, please this is not something I want to bring you into right now although I do want to address the situation with your stalker as soon as this issue is settled. The mission Alex is proposing is risky, and there are too many unknowns and variables. Not to mention, no one who sees me with you is going to believe you are just a model I am working with which will put you squarely in the crosshairs of several very ruthless groups of crazies."

Lainy could see Noah's mind was racing, and he was feeling torn, so she stood her ground and waited him out. It was easy to see how frustrated he was. She knew he felt as though he was being pulled in two different directions, but she thought the problem wasn't nearly as difficult to resolve as he seemed to believe.

"I grant you it might work—the plan that is—but the risk is too great. But then again, it would get you out of the country for a bit while Mitch and the team track down your stalker. Christ what a fucking cluster."

She held back her smile as he talked himself into the obvious solution. Stepping farther into the room, Lainy walked right up to Noah, placed her hand on his forearm and could literally feel the tension vibrating through him.

"Noah, please let me make my own decisions, okay? I have three older brothers who smother me already." She leaned closer and slid her hands up his arms and used the lapels of his jacket to pull him down, so she spoke directly in his ear. "I don't really want to consider you as another brother, I have something else in mind for you." Lainy felt his entire body stiffen and when he groaned, then cursed, the entire room erupted into laughter.

Chapter 9

I LAINA STRODE THROUGH the airport in Jos, Nigeria as if she owned it. Noah had to hand it to her, she was a seasoned traveler and hadn't complained about a single inconvenience—and there had been plenty. During their strategy sessions before leaving Colorado, they all decided the story would be the Nigerian government was trying to separate themselves from the struggles of their neighboring countries, and those efforts included a new publicity blitz, touting their efforts to safeguard and educate women as well as promoting their extensive efforts working toward wildlife preservation and management.

Alex and Zach's father, Daniel Lamont was still extremely well connected in the many parts of the world because of his years building Lamont Oil, so he'd been instrumental in securing their expedited travel visas. In exchange for their cooperation, the Nigerians had demanded sole use of the photographs that would be taken. The fact Noah Drummond was the photographer had pleased the Nigerian officials, but when they'd learned Ilaina had agreed to do the shoot for free, they'd been positively overjoyed. Noah had shaken his head at the *perks* they'd offered Ilaina, including an upgrade to a suite which in this part of the world often meant a private bathroom.

Seeing the public's reaction to Ilaina made Noah wonder how the hell she'd been able to survive the constant and intense scrutiny at each stop. Sure, he'd photographed most of the world's top models, but he'd sure as hell never traveled with them, and now, he was grateful for that.

Christ, every airport they'd been in had been a nightmare to navigate as her fans continually stopped them, asking her to pose with them and sign their shirts, books, hats—hell you name it, and she'd been asked to sign it. Through it all, she had smiled, graciously greeting people like they'd been her long lost best friends. It wasn't difficult to see how she'd gained a stalker. The more obvious question was how had she only ended up with one? When he'd asked her how she managed, she simply shrugged.

"You never want to burn a bridge because you never know when you might need to run back across it during the night." Her words had sent a shiver up his spine, and he hoped they weren't going to prove prophetic.

When they had finally checked in to their hotel, Noah had insisted she take a nice soaking bath while he'd ordered room service. They planned to be at their first location bright and early the next morning so they'd have the best light. Zuma Rock would be a spectacular backdrop for Ilaina's exotic beauty, and Noah was looking forward to the opportunity to take her picture in a public setting. After a morning of outdoor shooting, they were scheduled to visit the Women of Hope Ministries. The Nigerian government wanted to highlight their efforts to make their country safe for women, both residents and travelers. Even though it was purely a public relations manipulation, Noah and the Lamonts had agreed because it was a nice lead-in to their plans for the next day.

The day after tomorrow, they were scheduled to visit the nearby Yankari Game Reserve where they were supposed to "accidentally" cross paths with a group of Catholic Sisters visiting with children from their school. One of those children would be spirited away during their visit, then the real challenges would begin.

They'd flown commercial all the way so they wouldn't raise suspicion, but as soon as they had Myla, they'd need private transportation. The Lamont jet was currently on standby in Luxor, Egypt, awaiting his call. He planned to alert them in plenty of time, so they'd already be in the air by the time he and Ilaina were scheduled to meet Myla. The pilot would then be directed to land at Jos as soon as Noah contacted Alex via the secure sat-phone he was carrying. *It seems rescuing children is a lot more complicated than kidnapping them. Doesn't that just about figure.*

When Ilaina walked out of their suite's bath minutes after their dinner had arrived, Noah was completely stunned. How the hell did she manage to totally rock a pair of cut-off Levi's® and a cropped tank?

"*Cara*, you amaze me. I'm toast after all our traveling, and you walk in after a short shower, looking like the hottest woman on the planet." He moved to stand in front of her and lifted his hand to stroke his fingers down the side of her face, taking a moment to appreciate her incredible beauty. Here she was, halfway around the world, putting her life on the line for a child she'd never even met—that only added to her appeal.

"Come on, love. I need to feed you so you can get some rest." He kissed the end of her nose, and taking her slender fingers in his own, led her to the small table so they could enjoy the dinner that had been delivered moments earlier. Noah could see the small tells of exhaustion becoming more and more obvious as they ate in comforta-ble silence. Ilaina ate a large plate of fruit and raw vegetables and downed several glasses of water before turning in.

After his shower, he joined her in the large bed, pulling her against his chest and cherished the chance to hold her close. He relished the chance to just breathe her in and let her sweet scent settle his soul. He'd checked his email before coming to bed, and Mitch had sent an update on the investigation of her stalker. Both Mitch and Colt Matthews—the head of the Lamonts' security operation as well as a technological wizard—were working to identify the man who'd been sending increasingly ominous emails to Ilaina. Noah was pleased to know both men were working to identify the man. They all knew stalkers were notoriously unpredictable, often set off by small perceived slights, so they were taking the veiled threats seriously.

Noah had also read an update from Dylan Marshall, the local sheriff in Climax. Dylan had been a DEA agent before his cover was blown so badly, it had ended any chance he had of resuming his field career. The timing had coincided with his father's retirement as Climax's chief law enforcement officer, and Noah knew the locals had been thrilled when the younger Marshall decided to return home.

Dylan's email reflected his frustration with the slow pace of their progress, but Noah knew the bottom line was the Sheriff was just plain pissed off because several women had been hurt since he'd taken office—a fact his friend was taking very personally. Noah smiled; they had all teased Dylan he was going *Dom-Sheriff* on them, in other words, taking responsibility for the care of everyone around him, feeling like he should have gained control over the situation before now.

Noah hadn't even realized he'd finally dozed off until he woke up during the night to feel Ilaina's small, soft hand skimming his chest. Her soft fingers flexed in the hair covering his chest, and he fought to hold back a moan of pure pleasure. For several seconds, he wasn't sure she was awake, but then he heard her sensual hum before she whispered his name.

"Noah? Are you awake?"

Oh, hell yeah, baby—I'm damned well awake now. And evidently, your sweet touch woke up some parts of me before others. He had to hold in his smile for fear it would come through in his voice, and he didn't want to ever discourage her from waking him up to play.

"Oh, yes, I am indeed very much awake, my sweet *Cara*, and I can't think of any better way to be awakened than to feel your warm fingers caressing my bare skin."

Sexual desire was pulsing in the air around them, and when she pushed herself between his knees, he realized she evidently had been awake for a few minutes because she'd already stripped. The feel of her bare breasts sliding over his bare chest set all his nerve endings on fire. When she slid further down, hooking her fingers in the elastic band of his boxers, he moaned her name.

"I want to taste you. I want to feel your velvet covered steel as it glides over my tongue. I want to lick the ridges and veins as they shift against the roof of my mouth." Her voice was low and airy as she spoke to him. She quickly made good on her promise, and Noah found himself seeing stars as he fought off the climax threatening to end this interlude all too soon.

"*Cara.*" Her name sounded like a prayer, a benediction to his appreciation of her oral skills—and appreciate them he did. "Love, your mouth is going to be the death of me." The feel of her hot tongue lapping at his sensitized cockhead, wrapping itself around his girth before taking him in and sucking so hard, made him worried he was going to rocket right off the bed.

The overload of sensations was enough to make his eyes roll back in his head. When he finally managed to regather the fragments of his control, he pulled her off his cock and rolled them both so he was over her and inside her in a split second later.

"Fuck! Oh, *Cara*, my love. You are so hot and wet for me, baby. Your pussy is tightening around me as it tries to pull me deeper, but trust me, sweetness, I'm going to be as deep as I can get." With those words, he began fucking her in long deep strokes that had the tip of his cock pressing against her cervix and caressing her g-spot with each thrust of his hips.

When he felt her rock her hips upward, he knew she was getting close, so he picked up the pace and leaned over pulling her against him so she would feel him surrounding her.

"Mine," he growled. "You are mine, Ilaina. Don't ever doubt that. Carve the promise into your heart and know that's where it will stay until the end of time. Come with me, *Cara*."

He felt her pussy spasm around him almost instantly and caught her scream as he pressed his lips to hers. He only lasted a few more strokes, then followed her over the edge of a canyon awash in the light of pure pleasure. Honestly, it felt like he'd been launched into space. At first, there was darkness with nothing but a pinpoint of light followed by bursts of brilliant colors, then pure white-hot ecstasy riding on the back of his deep primal satisfaction of knowing he would be leaving behind a part of himself deep inside of the most amazing woman he'd ever known.

The next morning, they found themselves facing the

hot sun as they tried to take quality photos they didn't actually care about in front of a giant rock. While the structure was amazing to photograph from a distance—and he'd taken plenty—up close, it was pretty much like any other rock wall. Well, any other rock wall with one of the most recognized faces in the world gracing the front of it. Shaking his head, Noah worked to get the shots and was amazed at how easy Ilaina was to work with. He'd heard his colleagues remark about how she was easy to shoot, but he'd never met anyone with Ilaina Red Cloud's natural gift in front of a camera. She was at ease with a lens pointed in her direction, and it showed in each and every shot he'd taken. To say cameras of all sorts loved her was a gross understatement.

Their second stop was more inspiring and offered even more photo opportunities. The Women of Hope Ministries was operated by a small group of inspirational women who truly believed in their mission. Ilaina was a trooper, posing for literally hundreds of photos with everyone who asked her. Noah promised to send digital copies of the pictures to the director via email, so she could print them and share them with her staff and the women they served. He hoped to send them before they arrived back in the U.S. because no one believed the Nigerian government officials would be willing to share.

By the time they returned to the hotel, they were both in need of showers and food. After they'd both scrubbed away the day's sweat and grime, Noah and Ilaina enjoyed the dinner that was delivered to their room and began repacking their bags. They had deliberately packed only a few things in each of the bags they'd brought along so they could stuff everything into the bags that looked like photography equipment. They didn't want to tip off anyone that they weren't coming back to the hotel after today's shoot. They planned on picking up Myla and heading directly to the airport. Sensing the shift in Ilaina's mood, Noah walked up behind her and wrapped his arms around her.

"Are you alright, *Cara*? We can still cancel this you know? No one will think less of you if you decide not to go through with the plan." He knew his words weren't entirely true because Myla would be heartbroken, but Noah still felt as if he needed to give Ilaina an out if she needed it. She turned in his arms and looked at him as if he'd grown two heads.

"Are you serious? Do you really think I'd leave that child to the fate we all know awaits her? Please tell me you don't think so little of me." Her voice had gone from incredulous to hurt, and the unshed tears he saw filling her dark eye threatened to send his heart to his toes.

"No, *Cara*, please don't cry." He pulled her against his chest, wrapped in his arms and held her tight for long seconds, hoping she'd feel how much he loved her. He let her scent seep deep into his soul and realized this moment might well be more about his comfort than hers.

"I'm sorry, I wasn't clear. It just seemed as though you were unsettled, and I was worried you were having second thoughts. This is not your usual element, and I don't want you to do anything that jeopardizes your safety. Do you have any idea how important you are? The irony of me staying away from you for all this time in order to protect you from all of this, then putting you at the center of the storm the first time a mission comes up is not lost on me." Taking a deep breath, he continued to hold her in his embrace.

"Perhaps you are looking at this all wrong? Don't you

think it's possible fate might be trying to show you I'm stronger than you think I am?"

Her words went straight through him like a flaming arrow to the center of his heart. It had never occurred to him she might see his lame attempt to shield her from all he had been through over the years as a judgment she was weak. It humbled him that he'd been so very wrong about the most important person in his life.

"How is it someone so beautiful on the inside and the outside can also be so amazingly brave and wise as well? Now, let me start again. *Cara*, love, please tell me what you were thinking when your whole mood seemed to shift a few minutes ago." He smiled when she just shook her head and pulled back enough to grin up at him.

"Good save, Noah. I was just sad because I didn't even think to ask you what size Myla wears. I could so easily have brought her some nice clothes for our trip home. I'm usually much more considerate than this, and I feel horrible." He watched as her eyes once again filled with unshed tears before she added, "I didn't even buy her a gift."

Noah wanted to laugh, but he could see how sincere she was. What Ilaina didn't realize was being able to leave behind a life that had been nothing but one heartbreak after another was the only gift Myla cared about. She was putting herself in their hands without having any idea what her future in the United States would look like. The young lady who'd been treated with nothing but disdain since her father stopped sending money had no idea his family was coming to meet her in Climax.

After Myla's mother delivered her to the Catholic mission school, then simply turned her back and walked away, the heartbroken child had handed the nuns a note with both his and Alex Lamonts' phone numbers. It had taken the women a week to get someone to a phone with international access. As Noah explained all the details to Ilaina, he saw the realization light her eyes.

"She's just anxious to get out, isn't she? The rescue is the only gift she'd see, anyway. Noah, my heart breaks for her and for all the others we don't know about."

Pulling her close again, he spoke softly against her hair. "Your insight is inspiring, and the depth of your compassion humbles me, *Cara*. There are changes being made in this part of the world, but they are so few and centuries too late." He pulled back again and smoothed his fingers over her bottom lip, watching her eyes dilate at his touch.

"I promise, we'll take her shopping at our very first opportunity. Is that fair?" He was relieved to see her smile and nod. "Now, we need to get some rest. Tomorrow is going to be a big day. Drake Foster is meeting us tomorrow at the first site we've set up to shoot. Do you remember him?"

"Yes, well, we've never actually been introduced, but I remember he and Cash were on the same mission just before Cash met Layla, and I know that mission didn't go well. From what little Cash told me, he and Drake both had a hard time bouncing back. I didn't know he was still working for the Lamonts. I have seen him at Red Clouds a couple of times, but I've never spoken to him." She seemed confused by the fact Drake was here, and Noah was anxious to explain.

"Drake *asked* to help with this rescue. He and Cash didn't make it in time to save the young girl they were trying to rescue on their last mission. He sees this as a chance to do something to honor that child's memory. Alex and Zach agreed it would be a healthy step in his recovery. Cash found Layla—she has healed his heart. Drake needs this." This time her tears did fall, and he used his thumbs to wipe them away.

"I wanted to tell you tonight, so you wouldn't be surprised tomorrow when you see him. His story is you two were lovers, and he's followed you here to try to make up after a lover's quarrel. We're hoping it's a good enough cover, and if we need it, you two can provide some much-needed dramatic distraction." He nearly laughed out loud when he saw the mischievous grin spread across her face. She would know exactly how to play this one, of that he was quite sure.

"But just a word of warning, my sweet *Cara*. This plan is only *if needed*... and I would suggest you not make that act too convincing, my love because you do not belong to Red Clouds Dancing's resident surfer—you belong to me." He smiled down at her and crushed his lips against hers. His take no prisoners kiss was the perfect way to vent the frustrations of the day, the negative emotions draining away, replaced by the joy he only found in her arms.

Chapter 10

L AINY WENT FROM exhausted to sad, then straight to a rush of pure lust that felt like she was being swept out to sea... and it had all taken place in the span of just a few minutes. She had to give Noah credit, spending time with him was proving to be anything but dull. Seeing the sadness in his eyes when he realized how she'd misinterpreted his comment had almost broken her, but she'd resisted the urge to placate him. It was important for him to understand how she felt, and even though it was her nature to always be the *peacekeeper*, the Doms in her life weren't the only ones who believed they should begin as they intended to go.

Her brothers had always assumed she needed to be sheltered, often treating her like she was incapable of taking care of herself. Ilaina had tried to explain it to them thousands of times, and Cash had finally, only *very* recently, started to understand. It helped when she'd finally pointed out they did, after all, share the same DNA.

Collin had always been the most distant in his relationship with her, and she'd been pleased to hear him say one of his goals was for them to establish a closer bond now that their lives had brought them back together again.

As soon as Noah told her he considered her his own, she felt a surge of heated desire so strong, she was afraid she might well drown in it, and when his lips pressed against hers with unrestrained hunger, Ilaina was lost. The sensual feeling of his hands caressing their way up her ribcage was pure white heat, pressing in from both sides. When he moved his calloused palms to the undersides of her breasts, testing their weight, she couldn't hold back her moan.

He kissed with the same attention to detail that made his photographs works of art, and at that moment, her need for oxygen was placing a distant second to her need for his touch. For long minutes, they simply stood among the bags they'd packed, surrounded by a firestorm of lust-fueled passion threatening to spontaneously combust at any moment.

Ilaina was grateful she'd only donned loose boxer shorts and an over-sized tank top. The feel of Noah's hands skimming under her clothes was like an electric current setting every inch of bare skin he touched on fire. She finally pulled back because her moaned words were bubbling up faster than she could swallow them back down.

"Oh God, Noah... your hands absolutely light me up." *They make me think about the books I've read and wonder if all those feelings are really possible.*

Lainy wasn't entirely convinced she hadn't spoken the last words out loud and sure hadn't intended to tip her hand, but when he picked her up, she had to her wrap her legs around his waist, and the press of his rigid length against her heat sent another wave of heat to her sex.

"*Cara*, the feelings you've read about are absolutely true if the sub trusts her Dom to provide her with everything she needs. I would love to show you all the pleasures you have been missing." Oh boy, she wanted that more than he could possibly know, but first, she wanted this moment. She needed the emotional connection. She wanted the assurance he understood her need to be more than the woman whose face had never met a camera it couldn't conquer. Being *more* to this man was pure addiction. Pressing herself flat against him, she sighed.

"I want you to show me everything."

"And I want that as well—and I will, but right now it's about making sweet love to you. Tonight is about the euphoria of feeling my cock slide into your hot pussy and losing myself as you come all around me. There will be plenty of time to show you all of those decadent pleasures of kink—a lifetime as a matter of fact."

It was probably a good thing he'd picked her up in his arms because his words had gone straight to her heart, and she felt her knees wobble at the wave of need that had swelled up from her soul.

NOAH HAD INTENDED to talk with Ilaina about some of the "gadgets" Mitch had sent along, but when his kiss had caught fire, he quickly decided the discussion could be tabled until morning. He had been thrilled to make it through five different airports without being questioned about the specialty items Mitch had provided. God knew it would have been very interesting trying to explain the presence of such sophisticated tracking devices in among his photography equipment—particularly considering some of it was more than just a bit intimate in nature.

When he laid Ilaina down on the bed, he didn't waste any time helping her out of her loose clothing. Sliding his hands up her ribcage to cup her perfect, luscious breasts, he lowered his mouth to her rosy areolas and sucked first one, then the other until her nipples were both tight peaks. Her soft sighs and sexy moans sent shards of razor-sharp desire straight to his cock.

She'd surprised him when she admitted an interest in the lifestyle he had always known held the keys to his own pleasure. He'd never been a heavy-handed Dom, but the fulfillment he found when showing a woman all the ways he could bring her pleasure was more gratifying than his own release. He'd shared women in the past and had appreciated the ménages he'd participated in—helping another Dom show his sub the ecstasy of being the sole point of focus of two men was something he'd enjoyed on several occasions—but Noah felt a strong sense of possessiveness with Ilaina he hadn't anticipated. He wasn't sure he'd ever be willing to share her body with another man. He was certain he would never be able to share her heart.

"You never cease to bring the joy of the unexpected into my life, *Cara*. Knowing you are curious about what a BDSM lifestyle and The Club might be able to offer you is a turn on. We'll have an in-depth conversation about this, I promise you, but there are a couple of things I want you to know from the beginning. I'm not a sadist, and since I already know you aren't into pain, we shouldn't have any challenges in that department. I also want you to understand while I have enjoyed being a third for ménages in the past, I will never be able to share you in the same way your brothers or the Lamonts do Layla and Katarina." He moved up so that his hands were on each side of her face, his gaze intent upon hers.

"You are mine. I will never share your heart with another. I have loved you since the first time we stretched out on the hood of my car and watched shooting stars over the lake. Even though I've made some huge mistakes, my heart was always in the right place." When he saw the tears in her eyes, he knew he'd made his point, so he tried to lighten the mood a bit by adding, "It was just my head that was up my ass."

Ilaina's giggle was music to his ears, and he realized then just how much he'd missed by staying away from her for so long. Vowing to not waste another minute, he moved down her toned body, leaving a trail of kisses in his wake. Watching as the chill bumps raced over her light caramel colored skin, he smiled.

"You are so responsive. You are every man's dream in the flesh, and the significance of you laid out like a feast is not lost on me. Now, let's see how long you can hold back your release my love. No coming unless I give you permission."

Noah saw the panic in her eyes and smiled as he lowered his mouth to her wet sex. Running his tongue through the soaking folds of her labia, Noah didn't try to hold back his groan of pleasure, knowing the vibration would push her even closer to the edge. Her tissues were swollen and slick, and her body's involuntary efforts to press her sex closer to his touch were a heartwarming affirmation.

"You taste so fucking good. I could do this for hours, *Cara*. Feeling the petals of your pussy against my lips and the taste of your sweet cream as it spreads over my tongue saturating my taste buds is heaven." He saw her eyes go wide when he mentioned teasing her for hours, and as fun as it would be, he knew holding back an orgasm was a learned skill for any sub so he wouldn't expect her to hold off for long tonight. Not to mention the fact he was nearing the edge of control himself. Pushing his fingers deep into her, he felt the flutters along the walls of her vagina and stilled.

"*Cara*, hold it, and I promise it will be so much better. The longer you can delay your release, the higher you'll fly—trust me, love." When he saw her take several steadying breathes and quickly nod her head, he smiled. "Good girl." He curved his fingers up, so he was pressing on her G-spot, and her eyes dilated, and she started to shake. Just when he knew she was rolling over the point of no return, he commanded, "Come for me, *Cara*."

He'd quickly moved up and captured her scream of release before she brought them too much attention. Wishing they were back at home in his bed so he could enjoy the sound of her screams of pleasure as they echoed through the wide-open space of his home, he made a silent promise to them both that he would make that a reality as soon as possible.

Before she could come completely back to earth, he positioned himself over her and slid in as far as he could before she went over again and clamped down on him like a vice. Her panting breaths were about to rob him of the fine threads leashing his control.

"Oh God, I can't believe how good that feels. The ridges and veins of your cock caress me, and it is so much better than—"

He smiled when she seemed to realize she was speaking aloud. *Well, now wasn't that interesting? What are you not saying, my love?*

"*Cara*, I suggest you explain that statement... quickly." He'd stopped moving, making sure her eyes were locked on his. "Right now, love."

"Please don't be angry. I was just... um, well... the feeling of your cock is nothing like my vibrator."

He saw her eyes roll back and saw the mortification in them a split second before she closed them, trying to shut him out. He wouldn't allow her to hide from him, and there was nothing she could ever tell him that would shock him. Truthfully, he was beyond thrilled to find out how much better "real sex" was for her. More than once, he had heard women talking on photo shoots, and some had sworn their vibrators were better than their partners.

"Open your eyes, love." He waited for her to comply before he continued. "I don't want you to *ever* feel like you need to be embarrassed or humiliated by saying what you feel. I want to hear everything. Remember, you *belong* to me. That means I want it all, baby. Everything. Your thoughts, hopes, dreams, fears, aspirations, and love—I don't want you to hold anything back." He saw her eyes fill with tears but knew they weren't tears of sadness.

"You have touched my heart, Noah. I didn't think I'd ever find a love that felt safe. My deepest desire has always been to feel as loved as my mother does. There wasn't a day I can ever remember her not mentioning it to me. She always stressed I should follow my heart to the soul that touched mine."

Knowing he'd reached a place deep in her heart filled all the small empty spaces in his own heart with the warmth he'd always longed for. Relishing her tears as proof of their soul to soul connection, Noah leaned down and kissed away the salty sweetness of her tears as they trailed into her hair.

"That's it, baby—give it all to me." Resuming his measured strokes in and out of her slick heat, he knew he wasn't going to last long himself. When he felt her pussy locking around him, it triggered his own release. His balls tightened almost painfully before cum pulsed from the end of his cock, splashing against her cervix, pushing her closer to another release.

"Come for me, Ilaina." The walls of her pussy went slick with her honey, and the feeling was the most erotic thing he'd ever experienced. The added lubrication sent off a second firestorm midway through the first, and this one ran the length of his spine as bright lights dancing behind his eyelids telling him the lightning had reached the very depths of his brain. For several seconds, he felt as if someone had applied an electrical probe directly into his gray matter—his focus was destroyed, and he could barely breathe.

Rolling them to their sides, he continued to hold her in his embrace and let the moment's importance linger in the silence surrounding them. His biggest fear when he'd heard rumors of Ilaina's impending retirement from modeling had been she wouldn't return to Climax—the damage he'd done too great to repair. But he'd had Alex and Zach start looking for a place for him to set up shop, anyway as a leap of faith. And right now—holding her in his arms and enjoying the feeling of her relaxed and sated body as it rested against him, trusting him to shelter her as she slept—he realized the magnitude of the second chance he'd been given.

"Sleep well, my love. I'll hold you close and cherish the gift that is you." He knew her conscious mind hadn't heard his words, but he was hopeful her soul had heard and would believe his promise.

Chapter 11

T HE LOOK ON Ilaina's face the next morning when she'd looked over the *gadgets* Mitch had sent had been a Kodak® moment. Noah wished he'd been prepared and caught the incredulous moment on film. She'd been instructed on the various pieces she'd be wearing, and which ones were to be slipped to Myla as soon as they met her. The ShadowDance team had done a masterful job designing pieces that would look like the primitive creations of a child living in the poverty of a third world country. It hadn't surprised Noah at all to find out the Lamonts' friend, Ian McGregor had been instrumental in, not only the design but also in ensuring the pieces were finished and ready to be used on such short notice.

Noah didn't know Ian well, but his reputation as an innovative businessman was almost an industry legend. Ian had taken over his father's failing business when the elder McGregor died suddenly. From what Noah had heard from Alex, Ian had been in his early twenties, and with Daniel Lamonts' help and guidance, the young man had turned the business around in record time. Ian was also the sole owner of one of the East Coast's most prestigious BDSM clubs. Club Isola was located on a private island just off the Virginia coast and catered to Washington D.C.'s elite.

McGregor had gotten married recently, and Noah

made a mental note to send the newlyweds something as a gift and a thank you for the help with the tracking devices they all hoped would keep both Ilaina and Myla safe.

The road leading them to the Yankari Game Reserve was bumpy, and Noah heard Ilaina's soft groan when he hit a particularly deep rut in the road. "Something wrong, *Cara?*" He managed to suppress his laugh when he heard her growl from deep in her throat.

"I'm going to hurt him, you know? I really like Rissa, I swear I do, but she is going to have to make due with just one husband from now on." This time he couldn't hold back his chuckle. "It's not funny. I mean seriously, do you have any idea how mean I am going to look in the photos you are planning to take?"

"*Cara*, I promise you, you are not going to look mean, you are going to look sensuous. The only problem I'm anticipating is getting enough shots I'll be willing to share with the world. I can guarantee you every Dom in the world will be able to look at them and know immediately what was happening to you."

He'd told her the truth when he said he was going to have a hard time parting with any of the pictures because he knew the Ben Wa balls he'd slipped inside her this morning might be a great place to hide a backup tracking device, but she was paying a hefty price. If there had been any way to insert them after their arrival he would have waited, but he had studied the facilities at the entrance and knew there was nothing that would afford them that level of privacy.

"Remember, the ShadowDance team has worked several rescues, and they've heard it time and again. The first thing that happens is the women are stripped of their jewelry. Keep that lovely smile in place, *Cara*. And remember, there is a wonderful bedroom on the Lamonts' jet. As soon as we get Myla settled, I'll do everything in my power to help you feel better—how's that sound?" The look on her face was something between complete disbelief and fury, and he certainly didn't enjoy having it directed at him.

"Are you fucking serious? That's going to be *hours* from now. I need to come *now*!" Okay... so perhaps she wasn't coping as well as he hoped she might, but he couldn't very well just pull off the side of the dusty trail that served as the road to their destination and take care of her either.

"Well then, love, perhaps you should turn your beautiful self, so your back is to the door. Lock it and face me." He knew they were just a few minutes from the game reserve's check-in gate, but from the look of desperation in her lust-filled eyes, he didn't think this would take long. "Pull that pretty dress up and show me what is mine." When she quickly complied, he had to stifle his chuckle. "Good girl, now, pull those pretty panties to the side. Gorgeous." Christ, if he didn't watch where they were going, he was going to drive right off the road, and that would certainly attract more attention than they needed.

"Show me how you pleasure yourself, baby. I want to know exactly what you like, and I want to hear you scream my name as you come." He wasn't surprised to see her glance up at him, searching his eyes for confirmation. She must have seen what she was looking for because she quickly moved her fingers to her soaking folds. Ilaina's quick acceptance of his command spoke volumes about her desperation.

"You are beautiful, all spread out for my viewing pleasure. You've made me so hard, I can barely think because the majority of my blood is throbbing in my cock." Her breaths were coming in short pants, and he wished he could reach over and run his fingers through her wetness.

"Now, use your fingers to draw circles around your clit. It is already peeking out from under its hood, seeking attention. That's it, make the circles just a bit smaller. Now, give that ripe berry a firm squeeze and come for me, *Cara*."

Hearing her screaming his name was the absolute sweetest torture in the world. He wanted nothing more than to stop and lick away all her honey he saw streaming out of her pussy, but since it wasn't a reasonable option, he'd make due, giving her the handkerchief he pulled from his shirt pocket.

Noah hated that she had to clean herself up—as a Dom he had always considered that his responsibility and right. When he saw Ilaina start to put the soiled cloth into her purse, he held out his hand and smiled to himself as she reluctantly handed it over. Her eyes went wide when he brought it to his nose and inhaled the scent of her release and growled.

"This is just going to have to hold me over until I can get you alone, my love."

Once they'd cleared the entrance gate, he noticed they'd picked up a couple of tails and wasn't at all surprised. The government was likely trying to make sure they could get the best propaganda material possible, and he was fine with *that*—it was the extra witnesses to them spiriting away a child he could do without. Giving her a subtle signal to move closer so he could speak quietly, Noah waited for her to shift positions.

"We've got company now, and since we don't know how sophisticated their listening devices might be, we'll need to be discreet, *Cara*." She nodded her head in understanding. Smiling at him with mischievous intent, he wondered what she was up to and didn't have to wait long to find out.

"How much further to our first site? I'm anxious to get some great shots before we lose this light."

He grinned at her. Damn, she was something else. She was going to hit the ground running on this thing, and he was going to feel like a real ass for having doubted she could handle it.

"I've got a small map in the outer pocket of my bag. Grab it, and you'll be able to see the spots I've chosen. If you see something else you'd like to try, let me know, and we'll check it out." He knew she would understand if she happened to spot the school's bus before he did, he wanted her to speak up.

ILAINA WAS SO tired, she wasn't sure she had the energy to even get out of their small van again. They'd taken pictures at five of Noah's pre-selected sites and hadn't seen a hint of Myla's group or Drake Foster. No one had been where they were supposed to be, and she was hot and tired. Just as she was about to ask if they were going to have to give up, they rounded a small copse of trees, and the bus came into view.

Ilaina felt a wave of relief wash through her and sent up a silent prayer of gratitude. Suddenly finding herself re-energized, she was almost vibrating in her seat when they managed to park right beside the bus. She spent a couple of extra minutes freshening up her make-up to give Noah to have a chance to make contact and work out a plan with the sisters who were responsible for the group. As she was looking in the compact mirror, she noticed a truck pull into the small parking area and had to smile when she saw Drake Foster unfold himself from the cab. She didn't even want to think about how he'd known the exact moment to show up. Thinking about the balls in her pussy sending out GPS coordinates was just too weird.

The full scope of the sophistication of the team her brother and Noah worked with was finally beginning to soak in, and it was humbling to know how little she'd actually known about what they did. They took far greater risks than she'd realized, each and every time they went out, and it gave her a new level of respect for every soldier she knew was out there working every day trying to make the world a safer place.

Glancing up at Noah, she saw his quick nod and knew he wanted her to get out and engage Drake. *Showtime. Remember, a little girl's life depends on your ability to sell this.* Getting out of the vehicle with her usual grace, she stood and stretched, then turned toward the man striding toward her. Hoping she sounded surprised to see him, she sputtered, "Drake? Is that you? Oh my God... what are you doing here?"

"I'd say the question is what are *you* doing here, Ilaina? Although since you're with Drummond, I can probably guess it in one." She'd never been close enough to the man to realize how tall he was or that his eyes were the most amazing shade of crystal clear cerulean she'd ever seen. Lainy knew she had to stop staring. This was supposed to be a man she'd had a relationship with, so gawking at his eyes was going to be a huge red flag if anyone was watching.

"I told you this trip was important, but you didn't want to listen to me. These pictures are going to help the women and children's programs this country has initiated get some significant exposure. It's important attention and support this nation deserves for the changes they are making."

She walked away from the van as she spoke, Drake kept pace with her, the look in his eyes telling her she was doing the right thing, drawing eyes away from the van where Myla was hopefully, being stashed as they spoke.

"So, you couldn't have come with someone else? Christ, Lainy, you know how I feel about you spending time with him. Why him? Huh? Tell me." He'd halted her progress by grabbing her arm and turning her to face him. She played along and exaggerated her physical response, so it would look like he'd spun her with the unrestrained power observers would expect from a man of his size.

He was actually extremely gentle, and she could see the flash of embarrassment in his eyes at her reaction. They were far enough from the group he would be able to speak against her ear, and it would look like an attempt at seduction. He was facing the van and could easily see over her head, so he was able to give her a play-by-play. She tried to not react to the feel of his hand moving in slow circles over her lower back. She might have been able to stifle her groan if it hadn't been for those damn balls clanking together inside her. Now that she was standing still, and he was speaking against her ear and touching her, she was able to feel each shift and vibration.

"They are loading her now, so hang in for a bit sweetness. I know those balls have to be making you crazy, but you are doing great. That was one hell of a performance by the way. I'd tell Alex he should hire you if I didn't think Noah and Cash would have my head on a platter."

She felt a shiver go through her and wished it was Noah standing in front of her, so she could plead for what she needed. Drake pulled back and looked into her eyes but whispered his words just a breath away from her lips.

"Lainy, if you don't stop making those sweet little sounds and looking at me like that, we're going to have a problem, sweetheart." She saw him let out a shuddered breath before he shook his head. "I hope Drummond knows what a lucky bastard he is. Let's move. Play it up, baby, we're heading to the airport, and I want everybody thinking about you and me rather than the fact you are not going to use this site." As they neared the van, Drake leaned down and trailed kisses up her neck, and the moan that came from deep in her chest was all too real.

"Baby, I'm so glad we've worked this out. I'll follow you back to the airport, and we'll get your luggage then. Take some time and explain to your photographer friend that *friend* is all he's ever going to be. If you're going to be my wife, he needs to respect that boundary."

Drake spun her around just as they'd gotten back to the van, and she caught just a glimpse of Noah—the look of fury on his face nearly caused her knees to buckle. Drake pulled her flush against him, and the feeling of his erection was unmistakable. The feeling of his lips against her neck brought her back to the act she was supposed to be putting on, so she wrapped her arms around his neck and bit him lightly at the point where his neck joined his shoulder. She had to stifle her smile when she heard him mutter, "Fuck," just as Noah stepped up to them.

Chapter 12

N OAH KNEW THEY were acting. He'd known Drake Foster for many years, hell they'd shared women at The Club on more than one occasion, but it didn't matter—he still saw red. He'd nearly come apart at the seams when he'd seen Ilaina spun around to face Drake. There wasn't a doubt in his mind she'd overplayed it deliberately because he knew Drake would never manhandle a woman. Well, unless he had her strapped to a St. Andrew's cross or a spanking bench and her prior consent—then all bets were off. But watching what had appeared to be an intimate moment between lovers had been more than he could handle. Thank God, he'd had a very sweet young girl to hide in the back of the van.

Now, standing next to the "lovers," he waited for his friend to get his lips off his woman. When Drake finally looked at him, Noah didn't miss the gleam in his eyes. *Bastard is so going to pay for this.*

"Come on, Ilaina, let's go. We'll head back if you're done sucking face with your honey. I'm tired, and I need to get these shots processed so they can be delivered before we leave in the morning." He turned and stalked back the driver's side.

As they were leaving, he saw their tails still chatting up the nuns and wanted to make the most of their lead time.

He tossed his phone to Ilaina.

"Check the messages and make sure that plane is in Jos." When he heard her confirmation, he told her their ETA and had her text it to Mitch.

"He says we're going to be hot coming in. What does that mean?" Lainy was anxious to get to the airport. She'd feel a lot better when they were in the air.

"He is telling us the natives are restless, and we need to keep our heads up. We've attracted some attention we didn't need somewhere along the way, but it must be at the other end since our tails don't seem to be in a rush to follow us." He was still surprised he didn't see any dust behind them.

"Père, Sister Angel fixed those men's cars. She said you have some minutes to lead ahead." The fear he could hear in Myla's voice tore at his heart.

"Myla, you were such a brave girl. You've made me very proud. I'm anxious to get on that plane so I can hug you and introduce you to my girlfriend." He heard her giggle, and it was music sent straight from heaven.

"Remember what we told you, just stay put and try to rest a bit because you're in for a long ride on a very nice plane, and I know you are going to be excited by that. And by the way, doll, your English is really improving, you have obviously been practicing. Alex, Zach, and Cash are going to be very proud of you too."

They didn't hear any more from her and made the rest of the short trip in relative quiet. They were just coming into view of the airport when his Sat phone rang. He didn't bother giving his name because it was a secure line, and Mitch would know who was on the other end.

"Talk to me, brother, tell me we're clear—please." Noah didn't want to sound like he was expecting the worst, he knew Ilaina was hanging on every word he spoke.

"Things look good on this end, but I still want you to be watchful. Alex called in a couple of favors and well, those and a significant donation to the head of the airport's security detail seem to have opened the gates, so to speak."

Noah wondered just how significant that donation had been but knew neither Alex nor Zach would have blinked at handing over the money to save a child. Mitch gave them directions to the Lamonts' jet, and Noah was right in the middle of asking about Drake when Mitch interrupted him.

"Change of plans, boys and girls. We've got unknowns coming onto the field." Noah could hear the sound of Mitch's fingers flying over the keyboard. "Colt, I need an update on Drake." Mitch's words to Colt Matthews didn't surprise Noah. As the head of the Lamonts' security detail, he was no doubt in the driver's seat at that end. Colt's recent marriage to Jenna Lamont with their home being the newest wing of the Lamont mansion meant the man was basically on duty twenty-four seven.

Colt could match Mitch in computer skills, so Noah was relieved to hear he was also in the ShadowDance security control center more commonly referred to as the "Crow's Nest." It was obvious no one was taking any chances with their safety.

"He is the one coming in fast right behind them. ETA less than a minute." Noah was surprised by Colt's words, but when he checked his mirrors again, he could see the dust billowing like an angry brown snake up behind them. Mitch's next words were a welcome change in direction from where Noah had been worried they were headed.

"Stay on the course I gave you. When you get to the jet, load as fast as you can. Use the comm-unit we gave you, so we can stay in touch and keep Myla out of sight."

"Roger that. Jet is just ahead." He switched to the ear-bud piece. He wouldn't be able to talk to them, but he would hear if there were any major changes in the situation. "Myla, you awake honey?" As soon as he heard her quiet acknowledgment, he continued, "Okay ladies, here's the plan."

As soon as they pulled up by the jet, they were surrounded by team members who made quick work of unloading the van. They used an enclosed rolling cart to move most of the luggage—it also made concealing Myla much easier. Noah had been so damned proud of her. She had crawled into the cart without a moment's hesitation.

"Damn. She just stole my heart." Drake echoed the sentiments of all the members who had watched the brave ten-year-old as she stepped into the dark box without muttering so much as a hesitation.

Noah couldn't have agreed more. Seeing her eyes holding nothing but trust as he'd closed the door, all the while telling her to count backward from fifty, and assuring her that she'd be out before she got to zero. He'd managed to keep that promise, too. Opening the door and hearing her say ten had been a sweet moment indeed. As always, her smile lit up the room. He pulled her from the box and hugged her against his chest.

"Sweetheart, I can't begin to tell you how proud I am of you. I'm looking forward to hearing all about your adventure, but I need to help get things secured so we can get going." Turning to Ilaina, he continued, "Myla, I'd like you to meet Ilaina Red Cloud. She is going to help you get settled, then I'll introduce you properly." Placing Myla's small hand in Ilaina's made him smile because the child was obviously taken with his beautiful woman.

"Come on, Myla, let's get ourselves something to drink, I'm parched. Then we'll get ready for takeoff." They were already chattering like old friends as he hurried back outside to help.

They left both rental vehicles right on the steaming tarmac after Mitch assured them he had it covered. Watching as they lifted off, he wasn't surprised to see the van he and Ilaina had used and the truck Drake had used both leaving the airport. Glancing to his side, he smiled at the way Ilaina and Myla had hit it off. He and Drake laughed as they watched the two of them giggling like old friends.

"That's amazing. Truthfully, I was worried Myla would be upset by the scene Lainy and I put on, but she doesn't appear to have been affected. How can a child who has endured so much of the harsh side of life still smile and laugh so easily?"

Noah didn't have an answer to Drake's question. Mitch had said her paternal grandparents were coming to Colorado to meet her. They'd only learned about Myla shortly before they'd lost their son.

Several of the SEAL team members her father worked with had attended the memorial services for Mark Martin, and when his parents learned of Myla's dilemma and the impending rescue attempt, they'd asked to have a chance to establish a relationship with her when she arrived stateside. Unknown to his teammates, before his passing, the friend they'd known only as Marty was actually the son of a very wealthy oil company president. The Martin family could certainly offer Myla financial security. But it was her emotional security and happiness that concerned them all the most—the little brown eyed beauty had earned every bit she could find.

"Can you and the others take care of Myla for a bit? I

want to spend a few minutes with Ilaina." Drake's knowing smile and nod told him his friend knew exactly what he had planned.

"Absolutely. I agree she's earned a reward."

Chapter 13

I LAINA WAS ENJOYING her time with Myla, but the balls deep inside her were vibrating in time with the mechanical music of the jet, and she was getting dangerously close to imploding. She'd watched Noah and Drake as they sat chatting and decided if something didn't change in the next few minutes, she was going to excuse herself to the restroom and remove not only the Ben Wa torture devices but some of her stress as well. She tried to refocus her attention on Myla when she suddenly realized both Drake and Noah were standing in front of them.

"Myla, my name is Drake, and I'm a friend of Noah's. Would you like to meet the pilot? I think there are some very special treats onboard for you, what do you say we see if we can't track those down?" Drake leaned down, unsnapped her safety belt, and the little beauty scrambled out of her seat, quickly taking his outstretched hand. Lainy's heart nearly melted when Myla turned at the last minute and looked at Noah as if asking for his permission.

"Have fun, sweetheart, but don't you give away your heart to this big guy here, okay? And we're still on for our adventure report later, right?" Lainy saw the relief flash in the young girl's eyes as she realized Noah wasn't passing her off to someone else, merely letting her have a few minutes to do something new.

After they'd walked away, Lainy leaned over and kissed Noah sweetly. When he looked at her in confusion, she whispered, "That was for being her knight in shining armor. She adores you, you know?"

"I hope it's contagious." Noah wrapped her small hand in his so he could raise it to his lips, placing a kiss in her palm. When he pulled her to her feet and said, "Come. I want to spend some time alone with you, *Cara*," she almost came from his words alone. He led her to an elaborate bedroom, and when she heard the click of the door lock, she launched herself into his arms. She'd been holding back her hunger for his touch, but it was a losing battle. Feeling the strength and warmth of his arms as they wrapped around her, she let out a sigh of pure contentment.

"OH, MY SWEET love, you have been so patient, and I'm planning to reward you." He pulled back far enough to look directly into her eyes and wasn't surprised to see the desperate lust filling them. Noah knew she was skating on the edge, the balls pressing against her sensitive tissues had to be picking up the vibrations of the jet, but there was a shading of desire in her expression that told him it wasn't all about her need to be rid of Mitch's latest gadgetry.

"I'm going to tell Mitch what he can do with these you know… please, I really do need…" Her voice had taken on an airy quality, and the sweet sound sent all his blood south.

He loved the feel of her skin beneath his fingertips. The satiny smooth texture reminded him of cream filled coffee, the warmth glowed from the inside out. Her features were the envy of models the world over, but those who knew Ilaina Red Cloud knew the beauty she valued was what was inside... the spirit of the person was what she cared about. Noah had never met a photographer, model, make-up artist, or stylist who worked with Ilaina who had an unkind word to say about her.

"*Cara*, I know what you need, and I plan on taking care of you, right now." Covering her lips with his, Noah kissed her with barely restrained passion as he slowly moved his hands from where he held her face, following the gentle slope of her shoulders until he reached her upper arms. Pulling her tightly against his chest, he could feel her tightly peaked nipples pressing against him and struggled to hold back his groan of satisfaction. The light cotton dress she was wearing had done little all day to conceal the tightly peaked nipples as they stood tall and shouted for his attention.

Putting enough space between them so he could brush his fingers over the taut peaks of her breasts, he smiled into the kiss when he heard her soft, needy groans. He knew she was trying to be as quiet as possible, but he also knew her need to lose herself in his touch would soon win out.

"This room is soundproofed, love, so I want to hear your lovely voice. Each sigh and whimper belongs to me— don't hold them back." He gathered the dress in his hands until he was able to pull it effortlessly over her head and toss it aside. Opening the front clasp on her lacy bra with a quick flick of his fingers, Noah leaned down, drawing one nipple, then the other between his lips, pressing each of them against the roof of his mouth. Hearing Ilaina's sweet sighs made him long to speed things up, but she deserved to be well-loved.

"You were so very patient today, *Cara*, and I want to

reward you properly. Come, let's shower together, and I'll replace those metal balls with something I think you will enjoy more."

He managed to get them both into the spacious shower in record time after he removed Mitch Grayson's tracking devices and put them aside. Noah watched as Ilaina's entire body seemed to vibrate with tension. Seeing several soldiers he'd worked with exhibit the same symptoms, Noah knew without some kind of outlet for the adrenaline, her crash was going to be fast and hard.

Lifting her against him, so she wrapped her legs around him again, he rubbed the head of his cock through her slick folds before tilting his hips and sliding in to the hilt. Moving away from the wall, so the warm water caressed Ilaina's back, he lost himself in the feeling of her swollen tissues pulsing around him. As soon as he felt her frustrated attempts to shift against him, he pressed against the center of her spine, and when she arched her back, he pulled out and pushed in shallower this time.

"Oh God, yes... please."

Noah watched as Ilaina's eyes drifted closed, and her words were little more than butterfly wing whispers spoken to the wind. After several short strokes, he felt her lean back further, her body's silent plea for more.

"What do you want, love? Do you want to feel my cock pushing so deep, you feel as if we've become one?" Noah knew she was closing in on her release quickly and wanted to help her find the orgasm she was chasing. Picking up the pace of his thrusts, he was pleased when she responded immediately but didn't seem to be able to push herself over the edge. *Oh, my sweet love you are already attuned to your Dom, aren't you?* He thrust again, then again, pushing in as deep as he could and used the commanding voice of a Dom he knew she would recognize, "Come for me, *Cara*," just before he bit down on that tender place where her slender neck joined her shoulder.

Ilaina's response was immediate and volcanic. Her scream echoed in the shower loud enough, he was sure they were testing the limits of the master suite's sound-proofing. Mitch had assured him her responses wouldn't be heard by the others on the plane, and Noah had laughed at Mitch's offered assurance. His friend had also asked Noah to note how much a woman's ability to function would be hampered by the devices. Noah had chuckled after answering and suggested that Mitch do a practical application experiment using Rissa so he could see first-hand. Mitch had still been cursing as Noah hurried past the whining engines to reboard the jet.

Feeling her tighten on him like a steel band had almost stolen his own control and mentally reviewing aperture settings was the only thing that had drawn him back from the ravine's ledge. When he felt her breathing slow just a bit, he started thrusting in long, hard strokes and loved the feeling of the head of his cock pressing against her cervix.

"Shift your hips forward just a bit, love. Good girl, now use your fingers to draw circles around your swollen clit. Don't put your fingers on it until I tell you to. When I tell you, pinch it and remember, you're going to because it pleases me."

Giving her several seconds to climb the mountain again, he continued stroking in and out of her, varying the depth and the pace, keeping her on the edge. He relished the feel of her muscles rippling around his cock in ever tighter waves. The pulsing reminded him of the pounding surf along the eastern seaboard—the irony of both exhibiting the pure, raw power of Mother Nature wasn't lost on him.

A split second before he knew they were both going over, his harsh command filled the small enclosure. "Come for me, *Cara*." This time her orgasm wasn't as loud but no less intense. He was sure she'd stolen a piece of his soul, and he could only hope she'd understand it was hers to hold forever.

Chapter 14

I T HAD TAKEN two full days for them to make their way to Denver. They stopped twice for fuel, but he hadn't allowed Myla to exit the plane until they landed back in the United States. Even though they had secured all the proper travel documents for her, there was no reason to tempt fate and have her image pop up on a security monitor, alerting anyone looking for her location.

At their first stop in Rome, Ilaina had gone into the airport and purchased clothing for the Lamont triplets, her unborn nephew, and Myla. Even though she had explained she was trying to dilute the fact she was purchasing clothing for a young girl Myla's size, he'd teased her about cleaning out the airport shops as he and Drake had helped her bring an entire cartful of packages back onto the jet.

The joyful look on Myla's face made the time and money well worth it. Since Noah was currently Myla's legal guardian, he had persuaded Ilaina to let him purchase the clothing for the young girl, but she had insisted on buying her a couple of "special gifts," and he'd been thrilled to see one was a digital camera.

Ilaina insisted it was important Myla start documenting her new life from the very beginning. The thoughtfulness of Ilaina's gesture was a testament to her kind heart. Watching as Myla hugged her in gratitude, Noah noticed a scattering of the team members. Obviously, it wasn't *cool* for black ops soldiers to become sentimental.

There were several vehicles waiting for them in Denver, and they made quick work of transferring everything and hitting the road. Before they'd even gotten out of the city, Noah noticed Ilaina had finally switched on her cell phone and seemed to be scrolling through her messages. Something about her body language caught his eye, and when he glanced at her, he saw she had visibly paled.

"Cara? What's wrong?" He tried to keep his voice low so he wouldn't draw Myla's attention, but for the moment, they seemed to have her entertained with an iPad and a movie. Glancing over again, as soon as he could do so safely, what he saw in her expression had him pulling over at the next exit.

Once they stopped, he gently pried her phone from her fingers and scrolled through the photos that had been emailed to her. He quickly forwarded the entire email to Mitch and to his own email account. Noah asked Mitch to alert her brothers and the rest of the ShadowDance team as well. Even though he was nearly vibrating with rage, he did his best to stay calm, so Myla didn't become alarmed. It was their young passenger's inquiries that seemed to bring Ilaina back to the moment. She turned in her seat and smiled at Myla.

"I'm okay, sweetheart. Have you ever just been so surprised, you couldn't think of anything to say?" When Myla nodded, Ilaina smiled. "See, that's what just happened to me. My brothers will be happy to tell you, it doesn't happen often, so you should probably remember this day." They both giggled at Ilaina's joke, and Noah had to shake his head in wonder. Ilaina's ability to pull herself together so quickly was no doubt a result of years of being in the public eye—but it was still impressive to watch.

Noah knew Myla's grandparents were waiting at the Lamonts' to meet her. But it was going to be so late when they got back to Climax, the plan was changed to meet for a late lunch the next day, so they could all get a good night's rest. Even though they had told Myla her father's family was there to meet her, everyone knew it was in her best interest to have the added confidence sleep would give her. Ilaina had insisted she be allowed to help the little girl get ready, saying having her hair fixed and being dressed in something she liked would give her confidence an added boost.

When Noah drove past the road that would lead to Ilaina's home, she looked at him, questions easy to see in her dark eyes. He simply reached over and pulled her hand up to kiss her palm.

"Stay with me, *Cara*. I need to hold you tonight." It wasn't a question, he hadn't intended it to be. Her sweet smile was all he'd needed to know she needed his comfort as well.

Carrying Myla up to the guest suite, Noah noted there was a gift bag sitting on the dresser in the largest of his guest rooms he'd quickly readied for her before he'd left. Alex and Zach each had keys to the warehouse, and they must have let Katarina in to do some preparations as well. There were several outfits and pairs of shoes waiting to welcome Myla to the US. Ilaina helped him get their sweet guest settled and back to sleep.

Taking her hand, he kissed her fingers and whispered, "Come." He led her down the hall to the room he hoped they'd be sharing on a permanent basis very soon.

As soon as Noah's hand wrapped around hers, the warmth of his simple gesture filled her with a deep sense of contentment she hadn't even known was missing from her life. Walking into the master suite was like walking into a small floral shop. When Lainy stopped just inside the door and stared at the room, Noah gently tugged her toward the master bath. She didn't resist but was having trouble taking in all the beautiful bouquets and the softly glowing candles.

"Who did this, Noah?" She hoped the insecurity didn't show in her voice but knew it had when he came to an immediate halt and turned to face her. Threading his fingers in her hair, Noah used his thumbs to brush soft strokes over her cheeks.

"*Cara*, the flowers and candles are a welcome home gift from your friends. Alex and Zach have keys, and they inquired about what Myla might need. They also let me know Katarina and your other new friends wanted to do something special for you as well." He chuckled and pulled her close before whispering against her ear, "Alex and Zach wouldn't allow the women in our bedroom without my permission."

Lainy let out a breath she hadn't even realized she was holding. She noticed he referred to the room as *theirs*, but oddly enough, she didn't feel the need to argue the point. If he'd spoken those same words to her a few weeks ago, he would have felt the full force of her wrath, but now, it just seemed to settle her a bit.

"I'm sorry. I wasn't trying to be rude. The email unsettled me, knowing he was that close to me... that he took pictures of me with my family only emphasizes I'm putting everyone in danger by moving home. I'm having trouble figuring out what I should do, and I think I let my insecurity get the best of me. The thought of someone being in this room... thinking a stranger could have been in here... well, it just felt like a surge of ice water had gone through my veins. It's humbling to find out how vulnerable I've allowed myself to become." Lainy felt his entire body stiffen. He pulled back and lifted her chin, so she was forced to meet his gaze.

"Don't you dare let him intimidate you. You should be able to enjoy your family and friends' functions without fear, and I can assure you that is exactly how the entire ShadowDance team is seeing this. We'll have a sit-rep tomorrow evening, and you'll get a chance to see the full force of men who are at your back."

She felt some of the tension drain away and found herself taking a deep, calming breath for the first time since she'd opened the email and found dozens of pictures of her taken at her brothers' wedding and reception.

The last shot had been taken just seconds before Ilaina had come face to face with Noah at the edge of the dance floor, so she was sure her stalker would have still been there to witness them dancing together. She'd dealt with stalkers before and knew enough to not inflame them. Seeing her in Noah's arms was probably tantamount to waving a red flag in front of a bull. The thought she'd brought trouble to her hometown caused a shiver of guilt to race through her.

Leaning into the palm cradling the side of her face, she was so lost in the moment, she didn't realize she was giving voice to her thoughts.

"If he hurts you or anyone else I love, I don't know

how I'll ever be able to live with myself." Somewhere in the back of her mind, she realized she had just told him she loved him, in a round-about way, but she let the thought float right back out of her head because she was simply too tired to worry about semantics right now.

"Come on, my love, let's get you into the shower. I need to feel your naked body against mine. I do believe a couple of off the chart orgasms might ease your tension a bit."

She had been able to hear the passion and the smile in his voice when he'd spoken. The warmth of his breath and the brush of his soft lips over the shell of her ear sent a rush of moisture to her pussy. Suddenly, she was much more awake than she had a few minutes ago.

Chapter 15

S TANDING IN THE shower, watching the warm water run in sensuous rivulets over Ilaina's tan skin, Noah wondered if God had ever made any other woman as perfect as the angel standing in front of him. He leaned forward and circled her nipples with his tongue before teasing them both with stinging bites he knew would send fresh honey to her already soaking sex. Reaching over and pumping shampoo into his palm, he turned her so he could massage the shampoo over her scalp.

The stress he'd sensed earlier was evident as he slowly worked up the lather of shampoo and finger combed it down through the long strands of her dark hair. Massaging the base of her skull, he was able to coax the tension away with firm, circular motions. Using the hand-held shower-head, he was easily able to rinse her hair before massaging the last remnants of tension from her muscles as he rinsed the conditioner from the silken strands hanging to the top of her luscious ass.

One of the things about Ilaina that had defied all the usual expectations and parameters of world recognized models was she had abundant curves more reminiscent of the 1950s than what was currently considered the fashion standard. Moving her hair, so her back was now complete-ly exposed, he moved his hands up and down the entire length of her spine, using pressure from his fingertips to ease the last vestiges of rigidity from the muscles around her shoulder blades and on the tops of her gently sloping shoulders.

Stepping up, so the hair on his chest was brushing her bare back, he leaned over her shoulder and moved his hands into possessive positions over her lower abdomen and bare mound.

"Are you wet for me, love?" He already knew the answer, but he wanted her to begin to understand the importance of answering questions when they were asked. He used two fingers to draw lines of pleasure over each side of her slit and was pleased when her hips involuntarily tilted forward. When she didn't answer him, he gave her mons a quick swat.

"*Cara*, just because I adore you, doesn't mean I will allow you to ignore my questions." It was true, his love for her meant his expectations would be higher, simply because he knew how much deeper she could go, and how much more gratifying it would be for her if she would let her desire for his Dominance flow over her.

"Yes. I don't understand this, but I want to."

He smiled at the airy quality of her voice. She was so unbelievably passionate and responsive, it was going to be a joy to watch her find all the avenues the lifestyle would offer her. He had always known she was a natural submissive, but her trust would only be earned by a man she was willing and able to connect with on a deep emotional level. Ilaina had always been intensely connected to her spiritual side, something her grandmother had no doubt had a hand in. Noah knew each of the Red Cloud siblings had spent a fair amount of time with Níyol, but it had always been Cash and Ilaina who had seemed to connect with the Spirit

Talker the easiest.

It would be Ilaina's spiritual depth that would allow her to fully embrace the lifestyle he planned for them. He didn't want her to feel her submission took anything away from her. His belief had always been that when submission was freely given, it was a gift—a gift that should always be honored and cherished. He wanted nothing but the very best for her and planned to spend the rest of his life proving it.

"Do you trust me, *Cara*?" His question was a loaded one, and he knew she wouldn't miss that fact. He was more interested in her entrusting him with her heart than he was in her trusting he wouldn't physically harm her.

This time, she turned her head, so she was able to meet his gaze straight on. "Yes." There wasn't any question in her tone or her eyes, and the relief crashed through him. Noah knew he'd destroyed her trust in him years ago, and to have her state she trusted him again was music to his ears.

"I plan to make sure you never look back, my love. I want you to remember this moment in time and know this was when our journey together turned a corner." Stopping to kiss the tip of her nose and smooth the hair back from her heart-shaped face, Noah looked deeply into her eyes for long seconds before continuing. "But first, I think it's time for your reward."

Moving one of her small feet to the bench in the shower, he lowered himself, so he was kneeling in front of her. Using his thumbs to separate the swollen folds of her sex, he smiled when he saw her clit already peeking out from its hood. It was a deep pink and swollen with need—*perfect*. Leaning forward to lick a circle around the tight little bundle of nerves, he was pleased when she moaned, and the muscles in her thigh twitched beneath her tanned skin.

"Perhaps you should sit down on the bench, baby. I don't want you to fall." When she moved to sit in front of him, he brought her to the very edge and used his hands to push her knees wide apart. "That's right—open those beautiful thighs nice and wide, so I can see that gorgeous pussy. God, the smell of your arousal is the sexiest thing in the world, and the taste of your honey is the sweetest addiction in the world. I don't ever want to be cured of my obsession with you." He emphasized his last words with long licks from her puckered rear hole all the way to her pearly clit.

Using his fingers to pull open the wet folds, he was reminded why the ancients compared a woman's pussy to a rose opening in full bloom. He grabbed one of the small hand-held shower heads, looked up at her, and smiled.

"Keep your eyes on me, *Cara*. I want you to see the love in my eyes as I make my woman come." Noah knew she only realized what he intended to do when he switched the spray to a pulse. Her eyes widened an instant before he began moving it through her slick heat. Circling her anus, he watched as it tightened, then slowly seemed to relax under the massaging pulses of the water. Leaning forward to push his tongue in and out of her in a motion that was intended to mimic what he planned to do to her, he smiled at her moans.

"Like that do you? Tell me how it feels to be fucked with my tongue." Her voice was raspy, and he could hear that she was breathing in short panting inhalations.

"Oh, dear Goddess, I don't even know how to describe the tightness and how my whole body is almost vibrating with the need to come. I know it's going to be so good... that makes me want to chase it, but I also want to wait until you say to come because I know it will be so much more intense if I can wait. And well… I want you to be proud of me… oh… I can't… I can't wait much longer."

Noah felt the flutters of the muscles of her vagina around his tongue and knew she was rapidly closing in on the point where she wasn't going to be able to hold it back without help, so he pulled away from the smooth lips of her pussy. Using a dominant tone he knew she would recognize and respond to, he simply said, "Come for me, my love." He had just enough time to pull her clit between his lips and press down before she screamed her release.

He was glad he'd shut off and dropped the shower head to plunge his fingers back into her pussy because the sensation of her cream rushing over his fingers was something he was never going to grow tired of feeling. As she rode the first wave of her orgasm over the crest, he pulled her up, so she could wrap her legs around him and thrust in balls deep which sent her over once again.

As soon as he was inside Ilaina, Noah found himself immersed in a battle to hold back his urge to pound into her in long, deep strokes. Holding still as she milked his cock had to be the truest definition of "trial by fire" he'd ever known.

When he realized she was coming back down, he pulled her wrists together over her head and held them as he set a random pace of strokes, lifting her with his other arm, so he was varying the depths and angles. He knew she wasn't back to herself enough to control her climb back up the steep mountain of arousal and loved knowing she'd let go, submitting to his need to set the pace. Looking into her eyes as their dilated depths glazed over made his heart skip a beat—it was the most sensual thing he'd ever seen.

His father had once told him he would have to find the

right sub to truly understand the satisfaction of being a Dominant. When Noah had asked him to explain exactly what he meant, his dad had reminded him Doms only exist because subs allow it. The comment hadn't meant much at the time, but suddenly, the truth of his dad's words was crystal clear. Ilaina's words brought him back to the moment, and he regretted letting his mind wander.

"Noah, please... oh Goddess, please... I need you. I don't understand how I can need you so much. It scares me to need someone this much, but I need to feel your cock stroking me. Every time you push in, it's like the very first time and the feel of the ridges and veins of your cock kissing me on the inside is so perfect. The hard ring around your smooth head is so rigid, and the feel of it pressing so deep inside me makes me feel like I don't ever want you to stop. Oh my God, how can you light up my entire body from the inside simply by pressing against a certain spot?"

Noah knew he was already way past the point of being able to call back the release already starting to rocket through his entire body. When he felt her tighten on his throbbing cock like a vise, he was swept away with her over the edge into the blissful canyon of ecstasy.

Chapter 16

KATARINA LAMONT SAT on the edge of her chair, looking back and forth between her husbands. Being married to Alex and Zach was particularly difficult because they were both alpha males. Hell, being married to one Dominant man was a challenge, according to her best friend and sister-in-law, Jenna, but two Dominants could make a woman go postal without even batting an eye.

"I'm telling you, there is something wrong with that guy, Maxwell. There is just a lot of crazy-assed energy around him."

"Katarina, language." Alex's admonishment was expected but annoyed her, nonetheless. Why the man had such a hang-up about her cursing was anyone's guess, but she'd gotten a lot of spankings because of it over the past year and a half. It didn't appear she was making much progress on curbing the habit, but that was probably because spankings weren't really much of a punishment, in Kat's opinion. Zach leaned forward in his chair and looked at her thoughtfully.

"Kitten, can you give us something a bit more concrete to go on? Your concerns are really awfully vague."

She knew she was staring at him with her mouth hanging open, but Zach wasn't usually so… what was the word? Oh yeah… *stupid*. Did he really think she was so dim, she wouldn't hear the "oh great, here we go again" tone in his voice?

In the blink of an eye, her anger morphed into a deep hurt. Her battle with postpartum depression had been hard fought. It had taken her over a year to completely banish all the residual effects and seeing *that* look in Zach's eyes and hearing the condescension in his tone was hurtful.

Deciding not saying anything was by far the best choice, Kat stood and simply turned to walk out the door. Just as she reached for the knob, there was a soft knock at the door. When she opened the door, she came face to face with Mitch Grayson. Kat was well aware of Mitch's skill as a gifted empath, and that his sudden appearance was probably anything but a coincidence. Tilting her chin up, she waved him in.

"Hello, Mitch. They're all yours. I hope you have brought along rock-solid evidence to back up anything you have to say." She hadn't even tried to keep the sarcasm out of her tone, it wouldn't have worked, anyway. All she wanted was to leave the room and put as much distance between her husbands and herself as she could. Kat was careful to avoid touching Mitch, but he reached out and grasped her elbow.

"Katarina, are you alright?" It was a purely rhetorical question because not only was the man a Dom but his ability to *connect* with others, sensing their emotions and often their thoughts was well known. He stood perfectly still as he studied her for long seconds, his gaze never leaving hers. Kat tried to blank her thoughts like Rissa had taught her, but he only smiled and leaned close.

"Too late, sweetheart, and I'll be dealing with my love-ly wife for attempting to teach you how to do that." His smile told Kat he wasn't angry with either her or her friend

Rissa, but he didn't let go right away either. "I'm here to help, Kat." This time his tone was much softer, and she felt herself relax fractionally. "And for what it's worth, I agree with you about Maxwell Bradford. But like you, I don't have anything solid—yet."

Unshed tears filled her eyes, but she refused to let them fall. She wasn't going to let Alex or Zach know how much they'd hurt her feelings by discounting the concerns she shared with them. Bradford had visited their home several times over the past couple of weeks and had gone to great lengths to ingratiate himself with her husbands, but his avoidance of certain groups of their friends hadn't escaped her attention.

There was something about him that made the hair on the back of her neck stand up every time she was near him. And now, the same men who'd preached to her endlessly about the importance of trusting her instincts were the very same ones who had just discounted her gut feelings. Kat just gave Mitch a quick nod, letting him know she'd heard him and moved through the door. When she heard it close, she leaned against the wall and tried to regain her composure.

She knew the men in the Crow's Nest were likely sending her husbands alerts, letting them know she was still in the hall, but she couldn't seem to make her feet move just yet. Taking several breaths to calm her nerves, Kat mentally reviewed why she was so upset. Was it really because they hadn't listened to her?

Hell, even she knew her reaction was disproportionate to what had just happened. She'd been unsettled for the past several days but couldn't really put her finger on exactly why. Deciding she needed some silly toddler time, she turned to make her way up the wide staircase at the front of their home. Passing the front door just as the bell rang, she turned and opened the door and came face to face with Maxwell Bradford. His gaze swept over her, and she barely suppressed the shudder threatening to surface.

"Mrs. Lamont, how nice to see you again. I have an appointment with your husbands, but I'm a bit early." He took a step closer, and instinctively, Kat found herself stepping back away from him. When the corners of his mouth twitched, she realized her mistake. She'd played into his hand and shown him just how unsettled he made her.

"Well, Mr. Bradford, I'm quite sure the security staff has already alerted Alex and Zach you are here, so please have a seat in the living room. I'm sure they'll be with you shortly." Kat gestured to the room just to her right, but the man's gaze never left hers. The intensity of his look was intended to make her uncomfortable, and for some reason, that made it have the opposite effect.

She saw his eyes flick over her shoulder just as she felt Zach's arms surround her and pull her back against his chest. Breathing out a sigh of relief, she leaned into him and relished the feel of him molding himself around her.

"Maxwell, welcome. Head on down the hall, Alex and Mitch are waiting for you. I'll be along in a bit."

The other man nodded once and turned to make his way down the wide hallway leading to the office.

Kat felt herself release the breath she hadn't even realized she was holding.

THE MINUTE MITCH entered the office, Zach had known

their friend's sudden appearance was deliberate. Watching the exchange between their friend and Kat had been a lesson for both he and his brother. Mitch was a gifted empath, there was no question about it, but Mitch also had a way of talking to people that left them with no doubt whatsoever he was totally focused on them. Zach had often watched as Mitch won over people with that skill alone.

Before Mitch met Rissa, he'd been one of those Doms submissives regularly sought out. He and Alex had once asked Sally, one of The Club's regular subs, about Mitch's popularity. Sally had smiled and explained how important it made a sub in his care feel when he gave them his undivided attention. "He does the same thing to everyone he talks to, and anyone who makes you feel important draws others to them like a magnet."

Zach had thought about those words often but had obviously filed them too deeply in his subconscious recently because his sweet wife had just connected with Mitch after he and his brother had basically brushed her off. As Mitch's friend, he was pleased, but as Katarina's husband and Dom... not so much.

As a Dom, Zach knew one of the worst mistakes he could make was not providing the emotional support his submissive needed, and that was exactly what he and Alex had just done. Turning her around, he spanned her waist with his large hands and lifted her effortlessly, so she was standing on the second step of their home's ornate, curved staircase. The move put them almost eye-to-eye. Kat's personality was so large, he often forgot how truly tiny she was. He smiled at her before trailing his fingers down the side of her face along a line he knew was particularly sensitive.

"Kitten, I'm sorry." He didn't say any more because he knew she would know exactly what he was apologizing for, and he wasn't about to dilute the sincerity of his words with excuses or reasoning. When her expressive eyes filled with tears, he pulled her into his chest and just held her close.

Alex and Zach were both so in tune with their wife, they'd known she was pregnant before she had last time, and he was fairly certain she didn't know she was pregnant now either. She had been particularly emotional the past couple of weeks, and the dark circles marring the delicate, porcelain skin under her large blue eyes were a clear reminder that he and his brother had been neglecting their beautiful wife. They had both been working longer hours lately because they had several teams on missions, and time differences often made it more prudent to communicate with them during the hours after midnight.

Kat didn't sleep well unless at least one of them was holding her. She was often plagued by nightmares if she was alone. *Fuck, we promised ourselves our family would always come first and yet... here we are... ass deep in a swamp of our own creation.* Suddenly, he had even more respect for both their father, Daniel Lamont and their good friend, Trace Bartell. Neither man was a part of a ménage or polyamorous relationship, and Zach had no idea how they managed to keep their women happy and manage businesses that required very large time commitments.

When Kat didn't seem to be settling as quickly as he would have liked, he leaned over and scooped her up into his arms and started making his way up the stairs. Her tears had nearly been his undoing, but her words, spoken so softly against his chest almost brought him to his knees.

"I'll be alright. Please put me down. I don't want to

keep you from your business." It wasn't as much the words she'd spoken but the defeat and resignation in her voice that broke his heart. Zach didn't let her words slow his steps. He kissed her on top of her head, loving the feel of her wavy blonde curls beneath his lips.

"I don't think so, kitten. You and I are going to spend some quality time together, and we're going to do it right now."

Chapter 17

NOAH HAD FINALLY gotten Myla and Ilaina herded into one of his photo sets and was amazed at how quickly Ilaina had Myla posing like a pro. He chuckled at their antics but had taken hundreds of amazing pictures in a remarkably short span of time. Watching Ilaina nurturing Myla, bringing out her inner strength, he had to continually remind himself to keep snapping pictures because the metamorphosis was mesmerizing.

Ilaina had spent a lot of time making sure Myla's hair was perfect, and she was wearing something she was comfortable in. The young girl's physical comfort and confidence came through in every picture he'd taken. Noah had heard them talking upstairs and had nearly stepped in when he heard Myla hesitate to wear the dress she liked because she didn't think it was what he would want her to wear.

Myla had been worried the dress she liked wasn't good enough for pictures, but Ilaina had patiently explained the clothing was inconsequential. Ilaina had reminded her it was the way the garment made you feel that was important. She had assured the young girl if *she* liked what she was wearing that was what would show through and make the pictures perfect. After their photo session, they loaded up and were making their way up ShadowDance Mountain when he noticed both of his passengers had gone strangely silent.

"Myla? Honey, tell me what you are expecting today." His hope was that if she expressed what she was expecting, he'd be able to find a way to help her cope with the anxiety he could practically feel coming off her in waves.

"*Père*, I am expecting to meet the people who are parents to my birth father. The sisters at my school told me they live in the United States in a big place called Tex... um, Tex..." Ilaina turned in her seat and grasped Myla's hand.

"Texas. The sisters were right that is exactly where they live. I haven't met them either, so I called Katarina to snoop. She tells me they are really nice people." Noah smiled at Ilaina's reassurance. He hadn't known she'd called Kat, but he wasn't really surprised she'd taken it upon herself to check.

"I've spoken with them several times, and I have even visited their home in Texas." He left off that he had traveled the distance because it had been important that he see first-hand where Myla would be living. It was going to be hard to turn her over to strangers, but as Tori Bartell explained, he would likely lose a court battle since he didn't have any blood ties to the young girl.

"Can you tell me, *père*, what are their names? What should I call them?" He could hear the anxiety in her small voice and was grateful they were just passing the gate leading to the Lamonts' home.

"I don't know what they will prefer to be called sweetheart, but we'll soon find out. Please remember, Ilaina and I will be right beside you. Cash is already waiting outside for you." He glanced at her over his shoulder and saw her wide grin at his words.

Nobody knew exactly why the tiny girl had bonded with Cash Red Cloud—he was the largest and most intimidating of the SEALS she'd been introduced to—but there had been an instant connection between them that time nor distance ever seemed to dim. As soon as Noah had stopped his truck, Cash opened the rear door and unlatched Myla's seat belt to pull her into his arms.

"Pumpkin, I'm so glad to see you. I have been pacing out here forever. I should have known that ornery sister of mine would try to keep you all to herself." Myla giggled, and Noah smiled at the tender tone in the enormous man's voice.

"Well, hello to you too, brother mine. It's nice to see you. Me? Oh, I'm just fine and dandy... thanks for asking, your concern warms my little heart." Noah didn't try to suppress his grin because Myla was giggling at her new friend's comedy routine. "How was your honeymoon? And what did you bring me?" This time he joined Myla, and they laughed out loud at the incredulous look on Cash's face.

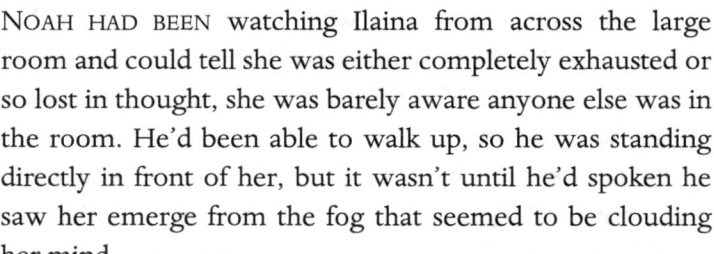

NOAH HAD BEEN watching Ilaina from across the large room and could tell she was either completely exhausted or so lost in thought, she was barely aware anyone else was in the room. He'd been able to walk up, so he was standing directly in front of her, but it wasn't until he'd spoken he saw her emerge from the fog that seemed to be clouding her mind.

"*Cara*, are you alright? You didn't even know I was near, and that is a concern, considering the security

questions surrounding you right now. Your lack of awareness is a bit troublesome, my love." He wasn't being
critical, rather he was genuinely concerned about her
safety. Noah pulled her close and ran his fingers over her
cheek and smiled when she pressed her face against his
palm like a kitten seeking the warmth of his touch.

The latest communication from her stalker had been
filled with promises of what life would be like once she was
with him full-time. The man's detailed descriptions of their
future together had been enough for the profilers they'd
consulted to construct age parameters and start putting
together a few socio-economic points as well. They'd also
said their real concern was the man was planning to kidnap
her and keep her secluded until she agreed to stay willingly.
So, it was imperative Ilaina remained fully cognizant of her
surroundings at all times.

"I know, I'm sorry. I don't know what's wrong with
me. I'm just so tired I can barely keep my eyes open. I
don't usually have trouble with jet-lag, but it seems to have
caught up with me this time." She tried to smile, and he
knew she was trying to alleviate his worry, but it wasn't
working. Taking a deep breath, she finally leaned into him.
With her cheek against his chest, her face shielded from the
others in the room, she closed her eyes and relaxed into his
embrace.

"Baby, we need to get you home. Come on. Let's find a
nice comfortable place for you to sit while I check on a few
things. I want to make sure things are settled with Myla
before we leave." She was barely awake by the time he set
her in a comfortable recliner, and by the time he'd returned
a half hour later, she was sound asleep.

Noah hadn't expected to be so long, but he hadn't
wanted to leave until Myla felt secure. They'd all been

thrilled the little girl had immediately taken to her paternal grandparents—well, at least she bonded quickly once they'd gotten her away from Cash. Everyone had laughed because it had taken his new wife pretending to feel slighted to get him to set Myla down. After arranging for Myla to spend a couple of days at the Lamonts', getting more comfortable with her grandparents before transitioning to living with them full-time, he made his way back to the sitting room where he found Ilaina curled into a small ball, sleeping soundly.

He was standing just inside the doorway, looking down at Ilaina—lost in the wonder of how truly amazing she looked and wishing he had a camera to capture the moment. He was so caught up in the moment, he hadn't even noticed Collin standing beside him.

"She is amazing, isn't she? I know the world looks at her and sees a perfect face and body, but I look at her and see the little sister I didn't spend enough time getting to know because I was so busy bossing her around." The emotion in Collin's voice surprised Noah, and when he turned to look at the man standing beside him, he was shocked to see he was clearly wearing his heart on his sleeve.

"She is amazing, but it's a beauty that shines from within. You would have been so proud of her when we went for Myla. I can't even begin to tell you how deplorable the rushed travel arrangements and shooting locations were, but she never complained. Her presence almost caused a riot in every airport we visited, yet she calmly signed hundreds of autographs and posed for a thousand pictures, her smile never wavering. I've never known anyone like her." Noah wanted nothing more than to tell her brother just exactly what his plans were, but Ilaina was a grown woman, and she deserved to be the first one to know he wanted her to be his wife—the sooner, the better.

"I hope you are planning to take her to your place to-night. We just got a call from one of the perimeter guys I hired. We had him on close patrol until I could do some upgrades on our security systems and somebody has managed to bypass my system. When he went inside Ilaina's apartment, there was a large vase of roses in the middle of the kitchen table with a letter detailing how her *fiancé* intends to make Ilaina the happiest woman in the world. It's a good thing I got the call because if it had been Cash, you wouldn't get out of here with her, Cash would have her under armed guard twenty-four-seven." Noah noted the affection in Collin's voice and had to smile at the truth of his words.

"But I've seen the way you look at her, and I know all about the security protocols you've installed in that fortress you call a studio and home. You need to get on the road before somebody alerts Cash. Alex said to tell you to use the Bat Cave entrance."

"Christ, I can't believe he actually got in your home. Do you have someone securing it now? I've got plenty of room if you'd like to stay with us tonight." Noah knew there was no way a Navy SEAL was going to let something like this keep him from his own home, but he wanted to make the offer, anyway. He was already moving toward the door with Ilaina cradled in his arms when Alex opened it. The two men walked them out, flanking them until Noah could settle her in and fasten her safety belt.

Alex nodded toward the road. "Let us know when you are safely inside the warehouse. We've got people at various locations along your route, but no one close to the entrance to the tunnel. We didn't want to draw unnecessary attention to that location. We'll video conference tomorrow at 1400, that will give our team plenty of time to get a few things in place. Colt and Mitch have a couple of ideas." Ordinarily, Noah wouldn't have let a comment like that go unchallenged, but the sly smile on Alex's face actually put him at ease. Alex had always reminded Noah of Hannibal, the leader of the A-Team. Not in looks, but in his ability to pull together a plan out of thin air at the drop of a hat.

Noah hadn't wasted any time getting down the mountain and was pleased to see the hidden gate was already open as he entered the cave entrance. He hit the remote that would close and lock the heavy metal door again as soon as they cleared it. He quickly made his way through the tunnel and into the secured underground of the warehouse.

All his security systems were still armed, so he was sure no one had made it inside. After parking the car, he turned to check on Ilaina and found her staring at him—her eyes were enormous. He didn't even have to ask if she had been awake when they'd driven through the tunnel because he could see the questions written all over her lovely face. Turning, so he faced her and taking her face in his hands, he leaned forward and kissed the tip of her nose.

"Come. Let's get you inside so you can ask all those questions I see swirling around in those beautiful dark eyes." There wasn't going to be any good way to break the news to her that the sanctity of her home had been breached, but it was necessary. Collin Red Cloud's words of faith in him earlier this evening were well-placed because protecting Ilaina would always be his primary responsibility.

Chapter 18

I LAINA HAD COME awake as Noah had been racing down the mountain. She heard him speaking softly into a blue tooth connection about everything being clear just before he swerved off the road and into a cave. When they passed a large gate, she saw Noah press the top of a small remote he held in his hands and watched in the rearview mirror as the large gate slid quickly back into place behind them.

She remembered Noah telling her his warehouse had an alternate entrance, but she hadn't expected anything nearly this sophisticated. The more she learned about this man, the more questions she had because it was obvious he'd been much more than a photographer and casual participant in the operations he'd referred to. When he pulled into the bottom level of the warehouse, she watched as the wall slid back into place as if it had never been opened. Staring at Noah, she saw the wariness in his eyes when he turned and noted she was awake.

Sitting at his kitchen bar a few minutes later, swiveling her beer bottle on the countertop in slow rotations, she painted circles of condensation and tried to wade through the palpable strain between them as questions raced through her mind. Noah sat next to her, and she could see he was watching her cautiously. She was certain he was simply giving her time to organize her thoughts and appreciated his patience. Taking a deep breath, she looked up at him, and even though she knew her smile was forced, she felt better for the effort.

"I barely know where to begin, Noah. Let's start with… why tonight? I assume someone at ShadowDance was on the other end of your quiet phone conversation. What I don't know is why it was necessary for you to sneak me back here." She looked up at him and saw his hesitance… but there was also a hint of sadness in his eyes, making her worry the information was so significant, he was concerned she wasn't going to handle it well.

"Before you answer, let me remind you I'm fairly bright, Noah, and I *will* know if you lie to me or edit the truth. My brother was a Navy SEAL, and I know more about what he did than I probably should because I did a lot of research. I'm not totally oblivious to the ways of the world, and even though I have traveled the world and have rarely seen anything to rival the level of security that surrounds my friends on this remote mountain in the Colorado Rockies—what I don't know is why." She saw the corners of Noah's mouth lift ever so slightly.

"*Cara*, the one given in this whole thing is everyone's awareness you are a very intelligent woman." This time his grin had been much more genuine, but he quickly sobered and took her hand. "I'll never lie to you. Your brothers might try the smoke and mirrors routine with you, but I promise I have always known exactly how quick that mind of yours works. Don't ever mistake my desire to protect and cherish you with underestimation."

Ilaina hadn't looked away from his eyes while he was speaking, and she was relieved to see nothing but sincerity. He didn't miss the unshed tears filling her eyes as she barely managed to rasp, "Thank you," before he took her bottled beer and set it aside. Pulling her to her feet, Noah led her into the large living room. He tapped the front of the music system on his way by, and the room filled with the soft sounds of Chopin's *Romantic Piano*. Turning her in time with the music, Noah simply wrapped his arms around her, pulled her close, and led right into a dance that was pure comfort.

"Dance with me, *Cara*. I need to feel you in my arms." When she would have stepped back, he held her tight. "No, settle a bit. I'm going to answer all your questions, I promise. This moment is for me, not you. I need to hold you and know you are safe."

Ilaina hadn't considered he might need to find the words to explain things... even though it made perfect sense once she'd considered it. Letting her questions slide to the back of her mind, Ilaina laid her cheek against his shoulder and let the music carry her away for a few minutes.

Noah finally leaned down and whispered against her ear, "Let's sit for a few moments while we talk." He led her to the leather sofa facing the rock fireplace. She watched muted versions of the fire's colors highlight his nearly perfect features as he patiently explained how the man who had been stalking her had somehow managed to circumvent her brothers' security system. Ilaina hadn't realized she was holding her breath until she was dangerously close to fainting. When she started to shake, Noah got down on his knees in front of her and placed both hands on the sides of her face, so her attention was focused on him and him alone.

"Breathe with me, *Cara*. That's a good girl. I'm sorry to be the bearer of such unsettling news. Collin agreed with me that you are safer here while this is sorted out."

He hadn't moved from in front of her, and she was grateful she still had him to focus on. When his words finally fully registered, she flinched.

"Oh my God, I'm putting everyone I care about in danger. I have to leave... *now*." Even she could hear the panic in her voice and hated how weak it made her sound. She'd never forgive herself if anything happened to her brothers or her new sister-in-law. Dear God, if something happened to her unborn niece or nephew... *I can't even think about that, it's just too much*. Everything was swimming in her view, and she wasn't sure if it was from tears or the fact she was losing her battle to fight off a full-blown panic attack.

When Noah pulled her focus back to him, she saw the concern on his face and regretted she had been the one to put it there. Taking several steadying breaths, Ilaina tried to smile but knew she had failed miserably. Feeling her eyes fill with a fresh flood of hot tears, she tried to blink them back, but they breached her lower lids and began a race to her chin.

She tried to use the unusual color of his eyes as a distraction. They were a strange combination of green and various shades of blue, and the depth of color always seemed to be determined by his mood at the time. When he was angry, she knew they would be almost Kelly green, but when he was sliding his length into her, his eyes were always a Caribbean blue. Her eye color never seemed to vary at all, so his had always fascinated her.

"*Cara*, I don't know where you have been for the past several seconds, but I'm pleased it must have been a wonderful escape."

The man's smile was devastating... it could literally light up a room. She had seen him use his smile with women of all ages, and the results were always the same—he could charm babies and the elderly alike. Lainy reached for Noah, and he took her hand and turned it to press his lips against her palm.

"Thank you for being so patient with me. I'm sorry I panicked, but the idea of harm coming to those I love is overwhelming. I honestly think it would be best if I just left Climax. I've attracted a few over-zealous admirers over the years and can tell you shaking them usually takes a long time. Their efforts tend to crescendo if they don't get results." She could feel her hands starting to tremble and it just plain pissed her off that she was scared... *again*. And now, her fears were compounded because the lunatic had gotten entirely too close to the people who meant the world to her. "I know you don't understand, but I really need to start making plans to leave Climax because—" Lainy's words were cut off by Noah's growl.

"No. You are not running. You have some of the best operatives in the world helping you. Do you really believe any of us would endanger your family? Do you honestly think you are safer *without* their protection?" She could see he wasn't about to let her leave and truthfully there was a small part of her that was terrified of leaving. He watched her for long seconds before asking, "Even if you managed to get away from me—which isn't going to happen—do you really think Cash would let you go?" He paused as his entire expression softened. "And you know what, love? I don't think you really want to leave. I think you know we can do more than you can do alone, but you are blinded by your worry and believe running is the only way to protect them."

He was right... on all counts. She tried to hold back the sob bubbling up from deep in her chest, but it wasn't possible. When he picked her up and took her place on the sofa, setting her on his lap, she buried her face in his chest and let all the tension purge itself through her tears.

Chapter 19

NOAH WAS WORRIED Ilaina was going to make herself sick. She cried so hard and for so long, he finally gave her a shot of Glenfiddich whiskey before stripping them both and moving into the shower. Setting it so they were surrounded by a slow misting rain and the soothing sounds of softly muted strings playing in the background, he hoped she would find her way out of the dark abyss she'd fallen into. Ilaina had never been one to let anyone see her pain, so the intensity of her response surprised him. Noah suspected this reaction was no doubt the result of a culmination of recent events, but he was still worried about its ferocity.

Feeling Ilaina's soap slickened body sliding against his bare skin was like a small preview of heaven. Her tightly peaked nipples were the deep dusty rose they always turned when she was aroused, and he loved how she moved against his chest, so the light dusting of his chest hair further stimulated her sensitive breasts. *Take what you need, Cara. Tonight is all about taking care of you.*

Ilaina Red Cloud's body was as close to perfection as any woman he'd ever known. As a professional photographer, Noah had seen more than his share of amazingly beautiful women, but there was an undeniable mystique to Ilaina. Her Native American heritage had provided her with classically high cheekbones and a unique elegance that can only come from a serenity of spirit. People of both genders and all ages were drawn to her like moths to a flame. Her movements were fluid and graceful—she'd always reminded him of a dancing angel.

Bringing his mind back to the present when the sensation of her wet heat enveloped him, Noah swayed on his feet as their souls connected. He hadn't planned to take her in the shower—he'd only wanted to soothe her. But every good Dominant knows plans must remain fluid because they are driven by the responses and needs of the submissive he is topping. And right now, seeing to her needs was far more important than following any preconceived agenda he might have had. When she had looked up at him with her tear-stained face and asked him to make love to her so she could forget everything weighing so heavily on her mind—even if for just a little while—all of his best intentions to let her rest had vanished in a white-hot flash of desire.

"Don't think about anything other than this moment, *Cara*. Let your mind empty itself into me, I'll take all those worries from your shoulders and give you exactly what you need. I've got you, baby." Covering her lips with his own, he felt the kiss go from tender to total raging possession in a few seconds. She was testing his control in every possible way, and he was having trouble just keeping his knees locked.

Ilaina had always pushed every single one of his buttons. She was sensual beyond imagination, her heart was as big as any he'd ever known and underlying it all was the soul of a true submissive. Her desire to put others first and to love those around her at all costs brought his protective instincts to the surface in every conceivable way.

Not even their passionate kisses could distract him from answering her request by lifting her into his arms and sliding her down over his aching cock. When he felt how wet and ready she was, he moaned against her ear.

"*Cara*, do you know how much it pleases me you asked for me to take you and your body had already prepared itself for me?" Knowing she had been willing to ask him to care for and love her in this way was a huge forward leap in the direction he'd been heading with her. And even though his heart had almost broken as he'd listen to her sob, there was a small part of him that rejoiced, knowing she'd turned to him in her time of need. The glimmer of hope that he was beginning to rebuild the trust he'd so foolishly lost a few years earlier made his heart sing.

"Please, Noah, I need you to make it all disappear for a bit… the worry and the fears for you and my family. I want to lose myself in your touch. Feeling you moving so deep inside me is the most amazing thing in the world." She certainly had that part right.

Ilaina was grinding herself against him, each rotation of her hips an exponential mind-altering pleasure. Her curvy body was wrapped around him as tight as the bark on a tree. Noah pulled her arms above her head, trapping both of her wrists in his hand, then leaned back. Watching her eyes widen and her pupils dilate with desire sparked a raging inferno inside him. Reaching between them to pinch her nipples, he smiled when she arched closer to the pain he knew was already turning into a soul-searing pleasure she wouldn't be fully able to understand. When she started speaking again, he noticed she was panting for breath, and her words seemed to be directed more to herself than to him.

"Everything sizzles… each stroke makes me want you

more. I don't know how to explain it and don't want to waste the moment trying to unravel it... this is a mystery meant to be experienced and enjoyed."

Her words might have been spoken during the heat of the moment, but he knew they'd been spoken from her heart, and they were enough to send the last vestige of control he'd been holding onto right down the drain, alongside the bubbles sliding off her peaked breasts like the world's sexiest waterfall.

"*Mine*," was all he managed to say before he set up a frantic pace of deep, pounding strokes. Gliding in and out of Ilaina's heat as her honey continued to flow was mind-bending, and her soft moans lit him on fire like a match to kindling. Just as soon as he felt the first ripples of her release, he tilted his hips, so the ridge around the head of his penis hit her G-spot with each stroke, then he watched—captivated in wonder as she shattered in his arms.

"Beautiful. In a lifetime I'll never tire of seeing you come, baby. Again." He had nearly growled his command for her to come again for him, and when she arched her back and screamed his name, the tiny sparks of electricity that had been teasing his balls erupted into a full-fledged bolt of lightning, shooting up his spine before reversing to streak back down to the tip of his penis as he emptied into her. Ilaina's second shout let him know she felt the hot splash of his seed against her womb's opening, and the satisfaction he felt at that was soul-deep.

Now as he stood beside the bed, watching Ilaina sleep, his mind drifted between his deep sense of awe and humility for all she represented in his life and how blessed he felt God had seen fit to give him a second chance to make her his own. The moonlight always seemed to seek her out, and tonight was no exception as it filtered through the tall windows of the master suite to pay homage to the Princess of Light, sleeping so peacefully in his bed.

When he was convinced she was sleeping soundly, he donned a pair of running shorts and made his way down to his office to check in with the ShadowDance team. He was relieved to hear there hadn't been any change since he'd spirited Ilaina out of the Lamonts' home several hours earlier. There wasn't any doubt in Noah's mind they'd eventually find out who was responsible for the break-in at Ilaina's small suite of rooms in her brothers' home. What he worried about was how much damage her stalker would do to her peace of mind before he showed his hand again.

Mitch had assured him he had successfully accessed her email and phone so she wouldn't be getting any more messages from the stalker Ilaina had nicknamed Crazy Craig after the Craigslist Killer. Even though the man seemed to be simply obsessed with having Ilaina at his side, so far, Noah worried his presence would quickly push the whole scenario to the next level. It was a concern other members of the team had also expressed to each other, but none of them had mentioned to Ilaina for fear it would reinforce her belief leaving Climax was the answer.

Just the thought of her being on her own—away from all the people who could watch out for her—sent chills racing up Noah's spine. He was sure she was aware she was in danger, but he wasn't sure she had a true grasp of how desperate an unstable personality's choices could be. Despite having traveled the world many times over, she'd always been surrounded by managers, stylists, representatives from the publications she was shooting for, and her own assistant. Taking off on her own would be entirely different, and he was sure Ilaina hadn't even considered the need to hire someone to handle her personal protection.

Noah grabbed his phone and quickly sent a text to Colt and Jenna Lamont-Matthews as well as Dylan and Melita Marshall asking for their help. Both women were experts in self-defense, and he asked if they would be willing to spend some time with Ilaina. Despite the late hour, he had four affirmative replies within minutes. *Damn, you have to love having kick-ass friends who are willing to step up and help.*

Through a flurry of messages, they arranged for the women to meet at The Club's gym the next day. Before he'd returned upstairs, Noah sent a brief summary of the situation to all three of Ilaina's brothers even though he was sure Colt and Dylan would be forwarding everything to them as well.

The photo portrait of Ilaina in his office caught his eye just as he was reaching for the light, and he found himself standing in front of it for several minutes. The shot hadn't been staged in any way but was by far the most sensual picture he'd ever taken. He couldn't think of anything he wanted more than to see that look of vulnerability and trust in her eyes again. Knowing she felt safe and secure in his love for her would be his most valued treasure.

Slipping back into the bed she was warming was the sweetest feeling in the world and one he hoped to make permanent in short order. Feeling Ilaina snuggle up against him like a kitten seeking heat made him smile. Wrapping himself around her as if that alone could shield her from every evil lurking outside his walls, Noah was finally able to drift off into the deep sleep he was only able to find when he held her in his arms.

Chapter 20

WALKING INTO THE gym behind The ShadowDance Club was like walking into an exclusive health club in any major city in the world. Lainy was amazed at the quality and variety of equipment. There must have been at least fifteen treadmills alone on one side of the enormous room. Two walls of mirrors made the huge room look like it went on forever. She could see a small lap pool at the other end she would bet was one of those where water was pushed toward you, so its length was inconsequential. The one feature Ilaina liked best was the kick-ass sound system. Noah escorted her through the gym's interior, pointing out the location of the women's locker facilities when Kat Lamont bounced in behind them.

"Hey, Lainy, welcome to the Alex and Zach's House of Horrors." Lainy couldn't help but laugh at the tiny, blonde bundle of energy. "Oh, you laugh now, but you'll soon see I'm not to be scoffed at. Jenna and Mia are wicked workout partners... well, they're easier than my husbands, but there's no sex as a reward at the end, so it's not really worth it." Looking up at Noah, Kat rolled her eyes and sighed, "You're not going to snitch me out, are you? Damn and double damn, that wasn't bad subbie talk was it?"

"Katarina, language." Lainy and Kat both jumped at the stern sounding voice directly behind them. "That's one, love. And of course, Noah would have told us you were cursing, we Doms have to stick together if we have a prayer of staying ahead of the bratty subs our club seems to attract lately." When he didn't think Kat was looking, he'd winked at Lainy, and she tried to stifle her giggle at his phony heavy-handedness.

"Are the other girls in the sparring ring?" Kat looked at Alex, and at his nod, she grabbed Lainy's elbow and started down the aisle between the weight machines.

"Katarina, Zach and I would like a word with you before you go." Lainy had known Alex all of her life, and she had only heard him use that tone a few times. It was a measure of speaking that she'd heard from her oldest brother a time or two as well. She'd always called it his SEAL voice because it was calm but laced with steel. Anytime Cash used it, everyone in the room seemed to freeze in place.

Kat's muttered "Fuck a duck" didn't escape Alex or Zach's ears. Evidently, Kat's more amiable appearing husband was just as intolerant of her cursing as his twin.

Lainy almost laughed out loud when she heard both men growl, "That's two."

Noah stepped up and assured Kat he'd make sure Lainy found the other women and let Jenna and Mia know why she'd been detained. Kat's face had flushed bright red, and she ducked her head before turning back to her husbands.

As Noah walked her from the room, Lainy asked, "Is she really in trouble? She really didn't do anything *that* bad."

"No, *Cara*, she isn't in that much trouble—although neither Alex nor Zach allow her to curse, it's an ongoing struggle as I understand it." He stopped and turned her to face him. Leaning close to her ear, he continued speaking so close, the warmth of his breath brushed her ear, and she felt her panties grow damp from the sensation alone.

"It seems Alex and Zach's sweet wife has a secret she herself has yet to realize, but you can't hide anything from a good Dom, love. They already knew their lovely wife is expecting, so they don't want her in the sparring ring. If I were you, I wouldn't expect her to make it in time for today's workout." He chuckled at Lainy's shocked expression. Smiling down at her, he moved his hands, so they cupped the sides of her neck. Using his thumbs to stroke the edge of her chin softly, he kissed her.

"Don't look so concerned, *Cara*. They are thrilled because they know Katarina always dreamed of having a house full of children, and you'll soon see, there isn't anything those two won't do to see their tiny tornado happy."

"Thanks for the heads up." She giggled and smiled up at the kind look in his eyes. "Now, can you show me where the other ladies are?" She found herself quickly whisked through a door and into another large room filled with padded mats and several women warming up. After Noah's quick kiss goodbye and warning not to leave the building without an escort, he turned her toward the others and with a quick swat to her backside, sent her moving toward the group.

"Hey, what was that for?" She looked back at him over her shoulder and let her eyes go wide in mock indignation.

"Just because I can, baby." Noah's grin was devilish and reminded her of all the times she'd seen that same gleam in his eye when they'd been kids. Moments like this reminded her of how devastatingly handsome he was, and the catcalls from the women in the room let her know she wasn't the only one that thought so. Shaking her head and laughing, Lainy turned to join the other women on the mat.

KAT COULDN'T HELP the knot quickly forming in her stomach when her husbands pulled her into a small office at one end of the gym. They hadn't said a word the whole time they'd been marching her through the main room, and the sound of the door snicking closed behind them when they'd entered the small room echoed in the uncomfortable silence. Deciding proactive was better than reactive, Kat postured herself with her feet planted a bit apart and her arms crossed under her now very sensitive breasts. *Damn. Surely, they don't know already? How could they? Hell, I only found out this morning.*

"Well, bossy husbands-mine... would you like to explain what this is about? I was going to work out with my friends as I'm sure you already knew. Now they're going to give me shi... um, trash for skipping the warm-ups."

Just for an instant, she saw Zach's eyes twinkle with humor before his eyes tracked to her chest and quickly changed to undisguised lust. Oh yeah, lust was good, she could cope with lust. *Fracking pregnancy hormones make me so horny. They'll probably be begging me to get out of here in an hour... or three.* In that instant, Kat felt her sex flood with moisture... damn her traitorous body, anyway. Couldn't it at least pretend to be blasé for a few minutes? When she chanced a glance at Alex, he was smiling at her like a cat that had corned a mouse.

"Katarina, my love, do you have anything you'd like to share with us?" He paused for that brief moment as he always did, and she swore it was for dramatic effect. *Damn, you'd think the man had been a freaking Broadway actor instead of a SEAL.* "I want to caution you, sweet wife, lying by omission is still lying. And we have plenty of paper to keep score."

And there it was—the proof they knew because during her last pregnancy they'd teased her unmercifully about keeping score of each and every infraction, so they could deliver all the punishments she had coming once the babies had been born. Never mind that after carrying triplets for all those months she'd then had an epic battle with postpartum depression. Do you think they'd gone easy and given her amnesty on all those damned punishments? *Oh hell no.*

Now, here she stood facing them… certain they knew she was pregnant, and she was still battling her desire to play innocent and deny her understanding. In the end, his intense expression and the shimmer of approval she saw in his eyes won her over, and she let the tears that had suddenly come upon her trail down her cheeks.

"How did you know? Damn, I wanted to surprise you this weekend. I had something special all planned too. Damn and double damn."

Zach stepped up behind her and pulled her against his length, and she had to fight the urge to grind her ass against the erection she could feel pressing against her back. Her husbands were both so tall, and she was so… *not*… their cocks often brushed far above their usual target.

Smiling to herself, she placed her hand over the one that Zach spread protectively over her still flat belly, and his whispered words against her ear melted her heart.

"Kitten we know your body better than you do and have known for a couple of weeks you were pregnant. And just for the record, we are thrilled with this news and can't wait to share it with the rest of the family."

Alex stepped up so she could feel the heat from his body moving over her skin in comforting waves just as Zach's was doing at her back. When he tilted her head back, so she was looking up into his eyes, the love she saw made her hiccup a sob before she turned and laid her face against his broad chest. For several minutes, they just held her while she cried softly. *Damn hormones, anyway.* When Alex finally broke the silence, she felt his words vibrating through his chest.

"Sweet love of mine, let's go back to the house. As much as I want to strip you and sink into your warmth this very minute, I want you to be comfortable even more. We've already arranged for the children to spend the evening with their grandparents in Colt and Jenna's wing, so we'll have our suite to ourselves. We'd like to celebrate our news before we share it."

Kat wasn't able to get any words past the lump in her throat, so she just nodded her head. She'd been feeling queasy for almost a week, and when she had gone to see Dr. Bree early this morning, she'd been surprised to learn not only was she pregnant, but she had lost several pounds and was anemic. She was feeling the consequences of both of those conditions now, so making a stand to work out with her friends didn't sound appealing at all, whereas the idea of a couple rounds of swinging-from-the-chandelier wild monkey sex that would leave her blissfully sated sounded divine.

As if he'd heard her thoughts, Alex leaned down, scooped her into his arms, and kissed her forehead as they made their way out of the gym. She was relieved to see they'd driven down through the gardens in one of the side-by-side electric carts the security staff used. Alex settled her on his lap, and Zach quickly drove them back up to their home.

"We really are thrilled, love. You're giving us another child to love… another piece of yourself and that is a gift no one else can give." She'd started to cry again, and he just smiled at her indulgently. "Let us love you, baby."

Chapter 21

J ENNA AND MIA had proven themselves to be tough
teachers. They'd all worked hard, and Lainy was relieved
to see she wasn't the only one dragging ass. It was easy to
see why the Lamonts' had nicknamed their younger sister
"The Warrior Fairy" because even though Jenna was
extremely petite, she'd become an expert in several types of
personal self-defense.

Lainy remembered hearing Cash talk about all the
team members who had foolishly agreed to spar with the
tiny young woman when they'd visit the Lamonts' home
on leave. She had rarely ever lost a match and had made
plenty of money on bets until word had spread fast and
furious through the ranks.

Leaning back against the wall in the showers, Lainy
listened to the other women chatter about children and
husbands, and for the first time, she wondered if those
things might be in her future. For so long she'd put her
dream life on hold to build a career that was only ever
intended to fund her education. Now that she'd accom-
plished both goals, she felt a bit lost.

Realizing how out of shape she'd become had certainly
been humbling. She needed to start utilizing the gym her
brothers had put in at home. Ilaina also vaguely recalled
Noah mentioning he had a home gym as well, so perhaps

while she was staying with him, he'd let her use those facilities.

She'd been lost in thought and suddenly realized that the locker room had fallen silent. Finishing up quickly, she got dressed and moved out into the gym's main room and noticed it was nearly empty. She saw the two former FBI agents she had been introduced to the other evening, a couple of the guys she knew from Red Clouds Dancing and another man she didn't think she'd ever seen before even though there was something strangely familiar about him.

Noah had told her the two FBI agents were former SEAL team members with Cash and the Lamonts. They were currently living in Texas and were visiting Shadow-Dance Mountain because they were considering going to work for the Lamonts full-time. When Alex had joined in their conversation, he'd added the ShadowDance team had been getting more and more requests for domestic security details, so that part of their business was expanding rapidly.

When the men in the gym looked up at her, she smiled and watched as the tall, blond man stepped forward and spoke to her.

"You're Ilaina, right? I'm not sure you'll remember, but we met the other evening up at the house. I'm Derek Lake, and that is my partner in crime, Joe Rivera. We didn't get to mention it to you when we met, but we worked a lot of missions with your brother. Don't tell him I said this, but he's was one hell of a SEAL, and we were proud to serve with him."

By this time, Joe Rivera had stepped forward and nodded his head in agreement. "For the longest time, he'd tell us you were his kid sister, and no one believed him." Both men chuckled, and Lainy couldn't help but laugh too. She remembered her brother telling her how his team hadn't believed they were siblings, so she had signed pictures for each of them and written a personal note on the back of each picture asking the man receiving the picture to take good care of her big brother.

"Please, call me Lainy, and I am pleased to meet you again. Have you by any chance seen Noah? He asked me to wait for him to return, but all my friends have already gone." Just as they had started to answer, her phone beeped with an incoming message. She gave her phone a quick glance before returning her gaze to the men standing in front of her.

Derek smiled and nodded. "The last I knew he was up in the Crow's Nest with Mitch and Collin. They were plotting some kind of mass mayhem, and since we are both still technically FBI field agents, we wanted to be able to plead ignorance, so we opted for a quick workout instead."

Lainy smiled. "That sounds about right. Well, if you see him before I track him down, please tell him I've headed up to the house. That message was from my mom. She's here visiting Selita and asked me to stop by before heading back down the mountain. I didn't even realize my parents were back, so I'd like to visit with her a bit." She turned to walk away and ran into Drake Foster's sweat-dampened chest. "Oh damn, I'm sorry. I didn't hear you come up behind me like a freakin' cat, Drake." All the men standing near her chuckled.

"Lainy, if you'll hang on for a few minutes, Jesse or I will walk with you. We won't be too long. Noah doesn't want you leaving without an escort." Lainy knew he was right, but her mom had said she wasn't going to be up at the house much longer when she'd asked Lainy to come up as quickly as she could, so she didn't want to wait for Noah's friends to finish their workouts and shower.

Glancing over at Jesse Hunt, she smiled at him when he nodded his head at her and continued bench pressing all the damned weights in the machine's stack... *good Lord*. It was obvious to Lainy none of the men were finished with their workouts, and she didn't want to be the reason they cut their sessions short.

Looking back at Drake, she said, "I'll make you a deal, I'll text Noah and tell him I'm on my way. That way he can meet me halfway." When Drake didn't look comfortable with her plan, she waved her wrist at him, adding, "Look, I'm wearing the bracelet Mitch gave me the other night, so if I have trouble, all I have to do is press the alarm. And then God and every Dom within a fifty-mile radius will get a memo detailing every personal secret I've ever had, *and* that I'm in trouble." Smiling to let him know she wasn't really being snide, she added in a calmer tone, "Besides, this compound is probably more secure than Fort Knox. Who in their right mind would try to come after me here?"

Even as she spoke the words, the hair on the back of Lainy's neck stood up on end. A small voice in the back of her mind noted that each time she ignored her internal warning voice, she'd regretted it, but knowing one of her dads had recently had some health concerns only added to her feeling of urgency to find out why her mom was so adamant about speaking to her. Those worries pushed all thoughts of her own personal safety aside.

She quickly typed a text to Noah and her mom, letting them know she was on her way. As soon as she'd hit the send button, Lainy said goodbye to the men she'd been speaking with and headed out the door. Before she stuffed her phone back in her backpack, she silenced it and didn't bother to check for incoming messages. She knew Noah and her brothers were going to have a fit about her leaving the gym. The men she'd just blown off weren't likely to be her biggest fans either once they talked with Noah or Cash. Lainy was so caught up in her concerns about her mom, dads, and the Dom patrol, she didn't notice she was being followed until the man she'd seen in the gym caught up with her.

Turning to face the man, she was surprised to see he was dressed in hiking shoes and jeans rather than the workout clothes he'd been in just a few minutes ago. When he moved to step in front of her, blocking her path, Lainy looked up into his face and frowned.

"Excuse me, I need to get to the house. My mom is expecting me, so I need to get going." Something in his expression was so familiar. she paused a few seconds longer and just looked at him. "I'm Ilaina Red Cloud. Have we met? You look familiar to me, but I can't figure out why?"

In an instant, the man's expression went from bland to feral, and Lainy took an unconscious step back.

"Why yes, Ilaina, we have met, in a hotel bar. You were quite friendly until I offered to buy you a drink and tried to kiss you. And you have continued to ignore me since you walked away from me that night. You have held steadfast in your refusal to get to know me—something I plan to remedy now." The empty look in his eyes caused a shiver to race through her. His gaze was so lacking in any kind of emotion, it was as if he wasn't even human.

Lainy was glad she had thought to put on the bracelet Collin, Mitch, and Noah had insisted she wear anytime she wasn't with a member of the security team. She'd teased them at the time about being a bunch of bossy old mother hens, but she was mighty grateful for their insight now. She managed to activate the alarm on the bracelet just as the man took hold of her arm. When he started to lead her off the pathway, Lainy dug her heels in and brought them both to a halt.

"Hold on, I don't even know your name. Why would I leave here with you? Where do you want me to go? My mom and Noah are waiting for me. If I don't show up at the house in a couple of minutes, everybody is going to be looking for me. How did you get past the Lamonts' security, anyway?" Lainy knew her voice had a tendency to go up in pitch when she got excited or scared, and the last few words she'd just spoken had sounded an awful lot like Minnie Mouse.

His grip on her arm tightened as he pulled her along beside him through the trees. It was taking all her focus to stay on her feet and keep the tree limbs from slapping her in the face, so asking more questions was going to have to wait. They headed down a steep slope, and when she slipped again, she dropped her backpack. When she finally managed to get her feet under her, she realized they were standing next to a large black pickup.

"Hey, I dropped my backpack, I need it."

"No, you don't. I'll provide you with everything you could ever want, Ilaina." His words were spoken softly, but they were hollow sounding. When he unlocked the truck and started to lift her into the seat, she began to panic.

"I have to have that bag. It has my medication in it. If I don't have that, I'll be sick within hours. You can't just take me to a clinic, you know. My face is not exactly unknown as I'm sure you already know. People will have heard about this, and the minute you walk into a hospital or clinic with me, they are going to have you in custody." When she saw he was starting to weaken, she knew to press further. *Wow…who knew having three older brothers to practice on all those years was going to pay off like this?* "Really, I need that bag, and it isn't far. See? It's just by that tree root."

"Fuck it. I'll get your bag for you, but don't you dare move. Give me any trouble, and we'll stop by and pick up that pretty blonde sister-in-law of yours on the way out of town. I happen to know exactly where she is thanks to Alex and Zach Lamont setting me up at the new motel."

He was gone from her side less than a minute, and Ilaina had remained as still as a statue. She had planned to make a break for it, but his words about Layla had turned her blood to ice—she would never do anything to hurt any member of her family. She knew Noah and the others would already be looking for her, so all she had to do was stay calm and give them a chance to catch up with them.

Suddenly remembering all the things Mia had mentioned during their training, Lainy decided it was time to start providing the Crow's Nest staff with some useful information since the bracelet she was wearing was not only broadcasting her GPS location, it was also relaying an audio feed. As he walked back up to her and handed her the backpack she'd dropped, Lainy tried to smile but feared it probably looked more like a grimace.

"Thank you for getting my bag. Hey, what do I call you? You haven't told me your name."

"Call me Max. Now, get in quickly and fasten your safety belt because we're going to be traveling over some pretty rough terrain." His voice was strained, and she noticed for the first time a telltale trembling in his hands.

"Well, Max, this is a beautiful pickup... and black is my favorite color too." Once he'd started the truck, she found herself fighting panic, and the black dots swimming in her vision weren't fading now that he was driving down a steep mountain trail better suited for a damned goat than a truck. For the first time in her life, Lainy was experiencing fear being in her beloved Rocky Mountains.

"Um... Max? Are you sure this trail is made for trucks? I mean, it seems a bit steep don't you think? I'm usually pretty hard to scare, I mean, I had three older brothers after all, and one of them grew up to be a SEAL and another a professional bull rider... so... well, you look like a pretty bright guy, so you can probably see where I'm headed with this, right?" Just then they hit a huge rock, and she found herself grabbing onto what her friends had always referred to as the "oh shit handle," screaming those exact words.

Just as she thought they were going to end up cart-wheeling the rest of the way down the slope, he seemed to regain control over the vehicle and turned sharply onto the highway at the edge of town. Without hesitation, he pushed the gas pedal to the floor, and within seconds, they were moving quickly away from Climax and everyone she loved.

Chapter 22

WHEN NOAH HAD gotten Ilaina's text saying she was on her way to the house because her mom was with Selita, he had been puzzled at first because he'd been in the kitchen just a few minutes earlier. He'd spoken with Selita but hadn't seen Cora Red Cloud. And then just as he'd walked back into the Crow's Nest and asked Collin and Mitch about it, the alarm on Ilaina's bracelet had been set off and all hell had broken loose.

Noah stood to the side and watched as Collin Red Cloud switched from worried brother to rock-solid professional in the blink of an eye. While Noah was grateful for the man's skill, he wasn't sure he would ever be capable of being so *detached* when it came to his *Cara*. Listening to the trembling in her voice as it wafted over the speakers, he'd been torn between relief she was able to provide them with great details and terror when he'd heard Ilaina's scream as the lunatic driving her down the mountain had apparently nearly wrecked the truck.

Just as he turned to sprint from the room, he heard Collin's voice.

"Drummond, sit the fuck down and answer phones. Get your head in the game man. We've already got all the team members we can manage out there looking for her. You'll be the most help to us right here." Collin hadn't even looked at him while he'd been speaking. Instead, his eyes had been moving between three different computer monitors, and Noah watched as the man's fingers literally flew over the keyboard.

"Is your mother in the mansion? Ilaina sent me a text saying your mom was with Selita and needed to speak with Ilaina immediately. That's why Ilaina left the gym without waiting for an escort." Noah had moved to the chair beside Collin and was surprised to see both Mitch and Collin stop what they were doing to stare at him open-mouthed.

Collin seemed to recover first. "No. Fuck, that means he's tapped into Mom's phone, maybe we can back into his phone that way and find out who we're dealing with." Collin glanced up as Colt Matthews moved quickly into the room. Taking a seat on the other side of Mitch, as the head of ShadowDance's security team, he was technically the one calling the shots now that he was in the security control center.

Noah had known Colt for years and had never seen the man fazed by anything, but he was obviously pissed yet another woman was being victimized on what he was going to consider his watch.

"Update me." Colt's clipped tone did little to hide his frustration. Noah could see the man was logging on to the computer network and was impressed he was obviously listening to Mitch's short summary of the situation while he typed on the keyboard and slipped on a headset that would put him in radio contact with every member of the team.

"Did you hear him tell Lainy to call him Max? Do you think we're dealing with Maxwell Bradford?" Mitch's question brought everything to a dead stop.

It was obvious Colt was considering Mitch's words just

as they heard Ilaina ask the man who had driven her off the mountain, "Where are we going, Max? And why did the Lamonts let you wander around their property? Did they know you were there for me? Why were you in the gym today? Did you know I was going to be there with my friends?"

Noah heard Mitch muttering exactly what had been going through his own head. "Calm down Lainy. We need you to keep your cool and feed us as much as you can. We've got eyes on you, but we need to know what we're walking into."

Noah also heard him muttering about needing to figure out a way to make two-way communication possible with the damned bracelet. Taking his first deep breath since the whole cluster began, Noah caught himself almost smiling at the incredible fluidity of Mitch Grayson's mind. Despite the chaos surrounding him, Mitch was still thinking about ways to improve the devices they were currently using. The man's ingenuity had saved Noah's ass on several occasions, and he was counting on it saving his woman's life this time.

Noah had begun to wonder if Lainy's kidnapper was going to answer Lainy's questions when he finally started talking.

"I was brokering a business arrangement with the Lamonts, and fortunately for me, they didn't listen to their wife's concerns about me." He'd paused for a moment, and Noah assumed he'd glanced at Ilaina when he continued, "Don't look so surprised. I really do pay attention—very close attention—to women. I knew Katarina Lamont didn't like me, and I'm equally sure she shared those concerns with her husbands, to no avail. Something she'll no doubt lord over them until you and I work this all out. Then you will be able to smooth her ruffled feathers and assure her I really am quite charming when given a chance."

"Jesus, Alex and Zach are going to go batshit when they hear this. How did his crazy-ass fly under our radar? And Jesus fucking Christ, there is going to be no living with Kat." Colt's voice was strained, but Noah could hear the smile underlying his words.

Noah kept answering calls as they came in, but grimaced when he saw Cora Red Cloud's number flashing on his screen. Answering, he wasn't surprised to hear the alarm in Cora's sweet voice.

"Tell me you'll find her, Noah. I know you love my daughter, and she loves you as well even if she has been too frightened to admit it yet." Noah's breath caught but before he could answer, Cora started to cry, and he heard her handing the phone off to one of her husbands.

"Noah? This is Julian Red Cloud. James has taken Cora to try to settle her a bit. I know you guys are busy, but we wanted to let you know that... well, we know you'll take care of our little angel. I'm not going to keep you on the phone, keep us posted, please." After he'd disconnected, Noah realized he hadn't even had a chance to speak. Shaking his head, he looked up, and Collin was smiling at him.

"Welcome to the family, Noah." Those simple words were all it took to calm Noah and bring his focus back to getting Ilaina back in his arms.

"WHEN ARE YOU going to tell me where we are going? I don't like driving down this highway so fast. Why are you taking me up Alpine Ridge Road? There isn't anything up here except a bunch of old cabins." God, she hoped the bracelet was working because if not, she was in deep shit. They wouldn't think to look up the rarely used road for days unless they were able to track her.

"Ilaina, I want to spend some time with you. We need to get to know one another if you are going to be my wife. We'll spend the night at the cabin, and I have a chopper coming tomorrow to pick us up and take us to the airport." Suddenly, Lainy couldn't catch her breath. The idea he planned to whisk her away to an airport via a helicopter was just too much to process, and she started to hyperventilate. She was barely cognizant of the fact they'd pulled up to the front of a cabin and stopped.

"See? This is why I wasn't going to tell you the plan. Now you've gone and gotten yourself all upset, and for no reason." His voice softened a bit, and he turned to her. "My lovely fiancé... I don't want to hurt you, I just want you to love me. You'll see soon enough, I'll be an amazing husband. I've waited for you my entire life. Following you around the world wasn't easy, you know. It took me almost two years to actually meet you."

Various events from the past two years began to gel, and things that had previously seemed unrelated slid into place like the pieces of a very complicated puzzle. Was it possible she hadn't had several stalkers but, in fact, had only had one? It wasn't that one Looney Tune crazy wasn't enough, but it also meant she'd actually been in more danger than she'd realized. She wasn't naïve enough to believe the man sitting across the truck cab from her wasn't far more malevolent than he appeared.

Lainy couldn't help thinking back on how many late-night runs for snacks or coffee she'd she made over the past two years. How many times had she assumed she was safe just because there were so few people in the lobby? She'd stayed in hotels all over the world, and now, she shuddered at how easily she could have been taken and never again seen any of the family she cherished so much. *Oh my God! I would have never known the truth about Noah.*

Lainy hadn't even noticed the shift in the weather until the silence in the truck was cut through by the howling of the wind. This winter had been one of those rare seasons that just didn't seem to want to let go. Almost immediately, the windows of the truck were being pelted with tiny balls of ice. Lainy hadn't lived in Colorado for many years, but she remembered well how unpredictable the weather could be... and how deadly it was when underestimated. She had considered trying to make a break for it when he moved toward the cabin but fleeing in these conditions in the lightweight clothing she was wearing would be foolhardy.

When she finally came back to the moment, she realized the man—who apparently believed he might be able to persuade her to marry him was watching her intently. His expression was so masked, his eyes so blank, it was almost as if she was gazing into nothingness. The man's total lack of affect was unnerving, and she felt herself once again shivering.

"Come on, let's go inside. I can see you are cold, and that means I am not taking very good care of you." When he'd looked at her this time, she saw for the first time what she could only assume was a fleeting moment of regret. He reached behind the seat and pulled out a jacket.

"Wear this, I know it isn't heavy, but it is better than nothing." She was surprised when he helped her don the jacket, then placed his hand on her arm. "Ilaina, I...well,

I'm afraid I've made a terrible mistake. I can see by your expression you are afraid of me, and that is the absolute last thing I ever wanted."

She saw him take a deep breath and let it out. As he exhaled, it was if someone had cut the strings that had been holding him so taut. Before she even realized what she was doing, she reached over and placed her hand on his, giving it a reassuring squeeze.

"Take me back, Max. That's all you need to do. We'll work out the rest, I promise." For the first time in over a year, she wasn't afraid of this man. A small part of her actually felt sorry for him... he looked utterly defeated. She was relieved when he started the truck and backed out. She refastened her safety belt as they'd made their way back to the highway, but she noticed he hadn't. It was obvious the road was becoming extremely slick, and she could feel the back end of the truck swerving. Just as she opened her mouth to remind him to fasten his own safety belt, she felt the truck begin to spin.

Hearing his curse and her own scream as they began rolling, all she could think about was the sadness she felt at not seeing Noah again. Burying her face in the overly large jacket Max had just given her, she heard herself scream Noah's name, then the only sounds she heard were grinding metal and breaking glass, followed by the eeriest silence she'd ever experienced.

Chapter 23

I F NOAH LIVED to be a hundred years old, he would never forget the moment he heard the unmistakable sounds of a vehicle being destroyed and Ilaina's haunting scream. He'd nearly stopped breathing when he heard her gasping, then screaming his name.

Every man in the Crow's Nest went completely still for just a heartbeat before pandemonium erupted. The bracelet was still transmitting sound and the GPS signal, so they knew exactly where to go, just no idea what they were going to find.

Colt was already giving the GPS coordinates to Dylan Marshall and his deputies. Dylan and Cash Red Cloud were closing in quickly on her location because they had already been en route to the cabin. Colt glanced over at Collin and Noah, and his one-word command, "Go!" was all it took to send both men skidding out the door and down the stairs. In less than ninety seconds, they were driving down the long drive leading to the highway. Noah was driving while Collin quickly entering the coordinates in the GPS system.

Noah's mind kept replaying the soft moans they'd heard coming over the speakers just before they'd left the Crow's Nest. That small reassurance Ilaina had survived the crash was the only thing he had to hang on to. When they rounded the corner near where the truck had left the road, Noah thought his heart was going to stop. He was very familiar with this area since his home was directly below them—almost a half mile directly below.

He knew the slope was steep and heavily wooded with one narrow ledge that would be wide enough for the truck—*if* they had been lucky enough the vehicle had stopped rolling at that point. Grabbing his climbing equipment out of the back, he took off running toward the sea of flashing lights up ahead.

Dylan looked up as he approached. "Gear up, we need you down there. We've got paramedics down there already, but they can't get her calmed down enough to winch her up." Noah didn't waste any time getting ready and had his line anchored and was scrambling over the edge in just a few minutes. Lowering himself down to the pickup, he could hear Ilaina's voice and noted she sounded confused and in pain. Making his way over to her, he leaned into the window and nearly threw up when he saw the mangled body of her kidnapper. It was obvious the man had died somewhere on their roll down the mountain.

"*Cara*, my love, let's get you out of this mess, shall we?" He tried to frame it as a question, but he also wanted to emphasize the need for action. It seemed to work. When she locked eyes with him, he saw relief wash through her expression.

"Oh God, Noah, I'm so glad you are here. That man over there wanted to marry me. But he knew he'd made a mistake and was bringing me back to you. I was so afraid I wouldn't get to tell you... hey, tell him to stop that." She was suddenly trying to bat away the hands of the rescue workers who were now quickly working to free her from the vehicle. Considering what he thought she'd been about to say, one part of him—the selfish part—wanted them to let her speak because he was anxious to hear what she had been trying to say.

"Baby, you need to let him cut you out of this mess. We're going to give you a lift out of here, okay? We need to get someplace warm so you can tell me all about your day. Your brothers are up top, and they're worried about you too."

He smiled when the mention of her brothers' worry seemed to settle her even more. Noah made a mental note to tell all three Red Cloud brothers about that because he knew Collin and Clay had often expressed dismay that despite their best attempts, their younger sister seemed to only respond to Cash.

Helping the EMS workers free Ilaina from the truck's mangled cab, Noah noted her right wrist appeared to be broken, and she moaned when one of the workers tried to roll her by touching her right shoulder. As they cut away the jacket she was wearing, Noah could already see the bruising from her shoulder belt forming a deep purple line diagonally across her chest. He'd be forever grateful she'd been wearing her seatbelt because the driver was evidence of what could have happened without it.

They had been attempting to block Ilaina's view of the driver's body, but she was too bright to have missed the lack of effort to treat him. Just as the litter was about to be raised up to the waiting ambulance, he saw big tears form in her eyes.

"Noah, I know what Max did was wrong, but he was trying to set things right. Can you, well… oh—"

Her words were cut off when the litter jerked upward. He quickly reached up and softly brushed the backs of his fingers down her cheek.

"I'll take care of it, *Cara*." Watching her being lifted

away from him was one of the most difficult moments of his life. He turned to the others who were still perched on the ledge, knowing they had heard their exchange.

"Go. We'll take care of things here and make sure we're respectable about it." Noah had known Deputy Quinn Tucker since they were kids and knew the man was good for his word. "If it will help Lainy rest easier knowing we're playing nice, then assure her we were compassionate as well as professional, but most of all—just get your ass in gear before that ambulance leaves without you." Quinn grinned and helped Noah quickly switch over his gear so he could be hoisted back up the side of the mountain as quickly as possible.

Noah was glad the sleet had stopped falling, and it seemed like the wind had died down a bit as well. Thinking about the love of his life dangling over the edge of a mountain in a litter in that weather sent a chill right through him. He'd been dressed much warmer than she was, and he was freezing his ass off. He came over the edge, and Cash Red Cloud started helping him out of his equipment.

"Go with her, man, she's asking for you. Give me your keys, Collin and I will follow you. Clay and Layla are already at the hospital waiting for her—along with most of Climax if my guess is right."

Handing his keys to Cash, Noah looked up and simply said, "Thank you," because he knew nothing else would ever be enough. Noah could only imagine what it cost Cash to let him ride with Ilaina. There just wasn't time to tell him how much he appreciated the gesture.

Hopping up into the back of the ambulance and positioning himself near her head, Noah concentrated on the soothing words he was whispering close to Ilaina's ear.

They weren't far from Climax's small medical center, but the ride seemed to take forever.

Wheeling into the covered area outside the emergency room, Noah wasn't surprised to see both Doc Woods and Dr. Bree Creed-Jantz waiting when the rear doors were thrown open. He stood back while Ilaina was unloaded and listened as the paramedics updated the physicians about her condition. Bree turned to him as they were moving Ilaina down the hall.

"Hang in there, Noah, I really think she's going to be fine. We have been monitoring her feeds since the team got to her." They'd reached the door of the examination room, and she stopped him with a hand to his chest. "It's ironic, really. This is the first time we've used the wireless and handheld technology her brother funded, and we were able to make a couple of critical adjustments in her treatment before she even arrived here. Make sure you tell him, please. I'll ask you to wait in the waiting room for a bit, this room is just too small for us to do our jobs if there are extra people inside." She smiled sweetly and disappeared inside.

Walking away from that door was torture, but Noah made his way down the corridor to the waiting room and wasn't surprised to see it was already filled to overflowing. Clay grabbed him the minute he stepped in the door and started asking questions faster than Noah could even process his words, let alone formulate an answer.

Katarina Lamont stepped up and placed her tiny hand on Clay's arm. "Clay, I think perhaps you need to slow down your questions a bit. You are overwhelming Noah, don't you think?" The twinkle in the petite blonde's eyes told Noah she understood the irony of her words since they'd been spoken to her so many times. Kat Lamont was famous for her rapid-fire questions and topic changes.

Noah nearly laughed out loud at the dead silence that immediately filled the room, and any other day, the dismayed expression on Alex Lamonts' face alone would have made Noah's day.

"Well said, love, even though I do find your sincerity a bit in question." Alex's voice sounded strained, and Noah wasn't entirely sure if it was from disbelief or the fact he was trying so hard to not laugh.

Looking over Alex's shoulder, Noah watched as Zach just smiled and shook his head. "And to think she is usually even harder to handle when she is pregnant. God help us all." His chuckle made it clear he wasn't really frustrated with his wife's obvious attempt to lighten the mood in the room. Clay Red Cloud hadn't spent years working the rodeo circuit and not learned to shoot from the hip and tonight wasn't any exception. The flirtatious cowboy persona surfaced in a heartbeat.

"Why, Mrs. Lamont, I do believe you are right, and since I've heard you are an expert on this particular topic, I humbly apologize. Your husbands are lucky men—beautiful *and* smart." When he raised the arm Kat was still holding and kissed the back of her hand, Alex and Zach both growled, and the entire room erupted into riotous laughter.

Cash and Collin walked in, looking completely baffled by the mood in the room. Once everyone finally quieted down, Noah explained what Dr. Bree had told him in the hall, including the fact that Ilaina's treatment had been significantly improved because of the technology her brother had recently provided the medical team now treating his younger sister. Collin Red Cloud had always been the most stoic of the brothers, but his eyes filled with unshed tears and Noah heard him whisper, "For the first time, I am truly grateful for the money I've earned."

Layla Red Cloud reached for her husband's hand as she spoke, "It's not the fact you've earned the money, my sweet husband… it's the fact you've *shared it* that has made the difference." After several of the people surrounding them voiced their agreement, Noah thanked everyone for their support.

He was turning to go back and check on Ilaina when Doc Woods walked into the room. The elderly Doctor always commanded the room with a quiet authority born of many years' experience. He was as ornery as he was compassionate, and the old man never forgot anything. Looking around the room, the elderly doctor's gaze moved between Kat, Tori, and Layla.

"You young people keep this up, and we're going to have to add on." Then the old man grinned from ear to ear. "Don't forget I still get pictures even if Dr. Bree delivers 'em."

He gave them an update on Ilaina, and Noah found himself letting out a breath he hadn't even known he was holding when he heard a broken wrist, a dislocated shoulder, a badly bruised torso, and a slight concussion were the worst of her injuries. Doc turned to him and smiled.

"Noah, I know you have held back from Lainy for a long time—and I understand why—but I'm telling you, son, best be getting over that waiting thing." The old fart grinned at Noah's puzzled expression and nodded his head down the hall. "Room 207."

Noah shook his head and laughed at his dad's long-time friend. After his parents had both passed, Doc Woods had appointed himself Noah's "substitute parent." Noah had appreciated the elderly man's counsel on a variety of business and personal issues that had come up in the past couple of years. Realizing how valuable sage advice was and how often he'd sought out his parents' input hadn't really registered until they weren't there any longer.

"Yes, sir. I intend to remedy that in short order, I assure you." Noah nodded to his friends and strode from the room, heading down the hall toward his future.

Chapter 24

Six months later

NOAH DRUMMOND GLANCED around the large gallery hall and smiled with contentment. The room was awash in twinkling lights that sparkled off the New Year's Eve decorations highlighting every flat surface. Watching as his friends mingled with former and potential clients, Noah couldn't help picking up the underlying energy that seemed to be pulsing through the room. There was something different, but he hadn't been able to pinpoint exactly what.

His gaze naturally sought out his lovely wife as she moved easily around the room. Ilaina's natural grace and easy rapport with everyone she met would be a huge asset in her burgeoning marketing business as well as his gallery showings. He rarely looked at her for more than a few seconds before he started wishing he had a camera in his hand. Ilaina had always been beautiful, but it was easy to see she was going to be one of those blessed women who seemed to get even prettier as they got older.

Letting his mind move back to their wedding a week earlier, he smiled at the sweet memory. Catherine Lamont had worked tirelessly, making certain the event was perfect in every way, and Noah had finally come up with the perfect gift to thank her for all her hard work. Now it was just a matter of getting Alex, Zach, and Jenna on board to make his plan a reality.

The portrait he had in mind of the Lamont siblings would be stunning, and knowing how much the three loved and respected their mother, he wasn't expecting it to take much to get them to cooperate.

Catherine was a gorgeous, former model who had given up a lucrative career when she'd married a young entrepreneur named Daniel Lamont. Together they had built a conglomerate of business holdings that Alex and Zach now managed. Daniel had acted as a both a personal and business mentor to several of his children's friends who had lost their parents for whatever reason. The elder Lamonts were also huge financial supporters of the local medical center and several shelters for battered women around the state of Colorado. They preached and lived by the tenet that those who had received the greatest blessings should give the most back.

When the eldest of Ilaina's fathers suffered a heart attack three months ago, Catherine had made it her personal mission to ensure Ilaina would get the fairytale wedding she'd confessed to her friends she'd always dreamed of. Neither Ilaina nor her mother had been available to be of much help because they'd spent every waking moment at James Red Cloud's bedside. Ilaina had explained everyone in their family considered James Red Cloud to be a rock-solid source of guidance and comfort and having him sidelined had been a wake-up call to them all.

Noah had never doubted that Cora Red Cloud was a submissive to her three Dominant husbands, but everyone had seen an entirely new side of the tiny woman since her husband's illness. The change in Cora had amused her other husbands, and Noah suspected that was largely due to the fact no one had seen it coming.

Cora had managed her husband's recovery with the tenacity of a drill sergeant. He'd even seen her clear out their condo in Denver when she thought James was too tired for company. Noah had been hard-pressed to suppress his smile when she'd leaned behind Ilaina one night as she was all but shoving them out the door, winking at him conspiratorially.

James Red Cloud's recovery hadn't been without its ups and downs, but he seemed to be on the mend now—and there was no doubt that it was in no small part due to his wife's devoted care.

Jesse Hunt and Quinn Tucker walked up and casually leaned against the railing next to Noah. He'd known both men for years and hadn't been surprised to find out they were both members of The Club when he'd returned home this past year. Knowing they shared their women and their penchant for really bright, spirited redheads, he had expected their interest in one of the Lamonts' new female team members. Noah didn't know much about Jazmin Edwards because Alex and Zach had both been uncharacteristically tight-lipped about their newest hire. What he did know was that she was beautiful, and when they had been introduced, Noah had noticed it seemed as though the woman was making an effort to avoid being in close proximity to men she didn't know.

"What do you two deviants want?" Noah knew his friends would hear the laughter in his voice.

"Fuck you, Drummond. You get the most photogenic woman in the world knocked up, and suddenly, you're King of the Planet?" Quinn's words made Noah snort out a laugh. Standing at six-four with a body builder's solid frame, Deputy Sheriff Quinn Tucker wasn't a man people overlooked in a room. What they often did miss was the man's killer sense of humor.

For just a second, Noah was too stunned to respond, and both men took advantage and burst out laughing. Jesse Hunt leaned close and spoke softly.

"No, it probably isn't that obvious to everyone, but Quinn and I pay attention to details. How far along is she? Because she is starting to show a bit—oh hell, never mind, that's not any of my business. I'll wait for the big announcement but congratulations, anyway."

"Thanks—I think. Now, what do you two asshats want? Because I'm fairly certain you didn't come over just to be all sappy about Ilaina's and my big *unannounced* news." Neither of his friends usually had any trouble cutting straight to the chase, so Noah was more than a bit curious about their intent. They both sighed in resignation, but it was Quinn who finally spoke.

"You still work with the ShadowDance teams, right? Or at least you're in the loop?" When Noah nodded, Quinn's gaze flicked to Jazmin before returning to the center of the room. "What can you tell us about Jazi?"

Noah worked hard to suppress his smile. He'd been expecting the men to zero in on the pretty redhead, but he was surprised they'd decided to make inquiries of him rather than their usual *in your face* way of dealing with situations. Hell, both men were honest and direct, almost to a fault, so obviously, their interest in the petite red-head was sincere—and wasn't that damned interesting. He'd known they'd been frustrated when their longtime submissive suddenly decided to return to California without warning. Noah hadn't heard all the details of that situation, but the little he did know had sounded like they'd been *played*, big time. Deciding his friends had suffered enough recently without him yanking their chains further, Noah opted for transparency.

"I know she was recommended by General Franklin. She is field trained as well as something of a cyber-crimes expert. Alex and Zach mentioned utilizing those skills, making her a 'Mobile Mitch,' and what exactly that will look like is anybody's guess." He looked at each of them, and when he saw nothing but sincere interest, he quietly added, "Okay, there is something else. This won't be in the public version, but Alex mentioned something about her having a story to rival Jenna and Victoria's. I know General Franklin was watching after her before she moved to Colorado, and he escorted her here personally."

At Quinn's raised eyebrow Noah added, "General Franklin is their Pentagon contact for all the work they do for the U.S. military. I don't know much else, but I know she was hurt—both physically and emotionally—by a man who is now serving time. But I do know this much—both Alex and Zach feel like she is under their protection, so if you have a genuine interest in her, I'd suggest you speak with one or both of them before getting too far into it." Both men nodded their understanding.

They all stood back looking out over the gallery, and Noah noticed both Jesse and Quinn's gazes seemed to return to Jazmin every few seconds. Noah hadn't really been watching her that closely, but now, he could definitely see she was more than just a bit skittish. She stood close to an outside exit and kept her back flat to the wall while continually scanning the room as if she was expecting an ambush.

When a young man from one of the local families moved close to her and appeared to be trying to engage her in conversation, Noah glanced at his sides and saw each of the men's eyes widen, then narrow when the nervous woman seemed to stiffen and flatten herself even tighter against the wall. Both men growled, "Later," and moved off in her direction.

Noah's eyes scanned the room, and his heart warmed when he saw Ilaina across the room, admiring one of the recent pictures he had taken of Myla when he and Iliana had traveled to Texas for a couple of days to visit last month. Feeling something brush against his arm, he glanced to his side to find Níyol at his elbow, smiling up at him indulgently. When he returned her smile, she pulled him down so she could place a kiss on his cheek.

"It warms my heart to see the look of love in your eyes as you look at my *yazhi*," Noah remembered asking Ilaina years ago about the nickname her grandmother used. She'd rolled her eyes and said it was the Navajo for "little one" because she was the youngest in the family.

While Ilaina had been busy with her family in Denver, Noah had taken the opportunity to spend some time with Níyol, and they had formed a tight bond. She'd posed for him, and Noah was thrilled with the results.

"The joy I see in her face tells me everything I need to know. And congratulations to you both." The older woman's voice was quiet enough she wouldn't be overheard, and the twinkle in her eye let Noah know she was well aware of their secret.

"You are too wise, *shimasani*." Noah had deliberately used her own Navajo word for grandmother, knowing she now considered him one of her own grandchildren. "My beautiful *Cara* knew she wouldn't be able to fool you." He pulled her close and hugged her. "Did you like your pictures?" When he looked into her dark eyes, lined with the wrinkles of wisdom and time, he was startled to see them fill with tears.

"They are perfect Noah. You not only captured my soul but also the soul of every Spirit Talker who has walked before me. You have worked a bit of magic with your camera, and I am honored." Noah had already been offered enormous sums of money for several of the pictures and planned to donate the money to charities benefiting the Navajo people.

"They will be here before you even have a chance to blink, Noah." *Hold up! Did she just say they?* "He will look just like his beautiful mama, but she will look like her handsome papa." Níyol didn't act as if she had just pulled the rug out from under him, and he could only shake his head and laugh.

"Does Ilaina know?" He hoped her grandmother hadn't told her because he wanted to be with his bride when she heard the news.

"No. And I won't tell her or anyone else your joyous news, but you best not wait too long because her family is filled with men who miss very little." She turned and smiled up at him. "You are going to be amazing parents and raising your children with those of your friends will be special indeed. And Dr. Bree is going to be a wonderful mother too, oh, but wait until they share their news, please." As she walked away, Noah couldn't help but chuckle. It was going to take him a while to get used to the woman's ability to *talk to the wind* and hear the future. Between Níyol and Mitch, ShadowDance Mountain was fast becoming the hardest place in the world to keep a secret.

Chapter 25

I LAINA WALKED UP to Noah and leaned against his chest. She was beyond tired, but their friends hadn't shown any interest in breaking up the party yet.

"I love you. I just needed to tell you." She loved the feeling of his arms wrapped around her. The past six months had been a contrast of the best and most frightening moments of her life. Her father's illness had been an eye-opening experience for every member of their family, but as frightening as the lesson had been... it had been incredibly valuable as well. James Red Cloud was the anchor of their family and seeing him lying in a hospital bed had reminded them all about how fragile life could be.

Just as Noah had started to speak to her, Alex stepped up to them. "It seems this is a pattern with us, and I am sorry to interrupt you once again. But I'm afraid my sweet wife and Victoria Bartell have conspired to liven up your gallery opening, Noah. And Níyol tells me that Layla is only a couple of hours behind them."

Ilaina hurried over to where the two women were sitting on the leather sofa. "Oh my God, this is so exciting. Are you two doing okay? How can I help?"

Kat looked up at her and grinned before her expression turned serious and her breathing started coming in quick panting puffs of air. Zach scooped Katarina up and started for the door, Trace Bartell had his wife in his arms and was right on his heels.

Bree Creed-Jantz looked at Ilaina and whispered, "I think you and I are up next, sister." Ilaina knew she had to have looked surprised and Bree laughed. "No, no one told me, but I'm a doctor, Lainy, so I recognize some of the early signs. I'll see you in my office next week, right?" Bree hadn't waited for Lainy's answer before she rushed out the door with her husbands, Jamie and Ethan right behind her like two mother hens.

Looking over at Layla, Lainy noticed her sister-in-law appeared a bit green. She saw Cash and Clay quickly making their way toward where Layla was sitting cradled on Collin's lap. Lainy reached her first and took Layla's shaking hand in her own.

"Hey sweetie, you doing okay? You look a bit pale."

Layla looked up at her with unfocused eyes. "I don't really feel that great. I've asked Collin to take me home. Cash went to get Clay and then we'll be heading out." Layla laid her head on Collin's shoulder. When Lainy looked up at her brother, she could tell he wasn't at all happy and was relieved when he mouthed the word *hospital* to her. She nodded once to let him know she understood and went to get a blanket for them to wrap Layla in because she had started shivering. Cash took the blanket as soon as she'd returned and had no sooner wrapped it around his tiny wife than she groaned.

"Oh, Collin, I'm sorry, but I think my water just broke. You better put me down, or you're going to get all wet."

Lainy didn't hear what Collin whispered in Layla's ear, but seeing the blush that spread over her sister-in-law's cheeks, she could probably guess. Just then, Noah wrapped his loving arms around her from behind and placed his hands protectively over her stomach.

"We'll be along in a little while. I want Ilaina to rest a bit before we head your way. Keep us posted, please."

Watching everyone making their way quickly out of the gallery, Lainy was amazed when it took less than five minutes for the entire gallery to clear out. The only people other than Ilaina and Noah still in the building were the clean-up crew from the catering company.

Lainy had wanted to protest when Noah had said she needed to rest before they went to the hospital, but suddenly she was very appreciative he'd known what she needed even when she hadn't. Turning in his arms, she laid her cheek against his chest and just breathed him in.

"Thank you," was all she managed to get out before she felt the tears start to fall.

"You're welcome, *Cara*." He picked her up and made his way up the winding stairway, then down the hall to their room. By the time he'd set her on her feet beside the bed, her eyelids were starting to drift closed but with every touch... every brush of his warm hands over her bare skin as he stripped her, he was setting every nerve ending in her body on fire. She hadn't had any morning sickness, and despite the fatigue she'd been battling, her libido seemed to be soaring. She remembered listening to her friends discussing the side benefits of pregnancy hormones but hadn't really considered they were telling the truth until the past couple of weeks.

Lainy moved her fingers to the buttons on Noah's shirt and began exposing his muscular chest and kissing each new inch as it came into view. "Please...," was all it had taken to elicit a deep growl from him.

"*Cara*, I wanted you to rest, but I can see you are not going to do that without being thoroughly fucked are you?" Noah knew that Lainy loved his crude words, he could literally smell her arousal as her honey flooded the soft folds of her sex. Reaching between her legs, he circled his fingers through the slick lips of her labia. "Oh, my sweet wife, you are dripping wet at the thought of me pounding my aching cock into you. There is nothing sexier and nothing that pleases me more than knowing you are ready for me."

KISSING NOAH HAD always been an almost orgasmic experience itself, and this afternoon was certainly no exception. His kisses always set the stage, and when he spoke against her ear, she almost came. Now that he was seducing her mouth with his tongue, she wasn't sure she was going to be able to hold back her release, but proving again he was attuned to her needs and knew her body as well as she knew it herself, he pulled back just as she'd been ready to let go.

"No, love, not yet. I want to be inside you when you release all that pressure building up between those beautiful thighs." She must have had a surprised expression because he laughed out loud before continuing. "Oh, my sweet *Cara*, I have known all afternoon how needy you were. Even when you don't know I'm watching you, I'm with you. Even when my hands aren't moving over the softness of your beautiful skin, I am touching you—all you have to do is stop and *feel me* because I am a part of you just as you are a part of me."

Lainy felt her pussy pulsing, and before she could take her next breath, Noah had turned her, bending her over the edge of the bed and rained heated swats her on ass, alternating sides and intensity until the burning left by his palm turned to a consuming need that was almost more than she could stand. Just when she'd been ready to beg, he thrust himself inside her. She hadn't even realized he'd finished opening his pants, she'd been so lost in his words and how the pain magically seemed to change from hot to sweet.

Feeling the tip of his cock pressing against her cervix and the rigid ring of the corona massaging the walls of her channel made her breath hitch as she screamed out her release. Clenching her fists in the coverlet on the bed, Lainy was floating in the afterglow of a mind shattering orgasm, but the steady slide of Noah's cock in and out was quickly bringing her body back up in preparation for another free-fall into ecstasy.

"Ilaina, tell me how it feels. Do you relish feeling the power of our joining? Do you know how beautiful you are bent over so I can watch my cock slide so deep inside you, I can barely tell where you end and I begin? Seeing my cock emerge from inside your sweet body coated with your slick honey and framed by my handprints covering your beautiful ass is such a turn on, I can barely wrap my head around it. Knowing your body desires mine as much as I crave yours pulls my soul deeper into love with each stroke." Lainy felt her body starting to come apart once again, and just as she opened her mouth to scream his name, he ground out, "Come with me, *Cara*."

Noah tilted his hips at the exact moment he command-ed her release, and she was lost. His shout of release sent her even higher, and the fireworks she saw behind her tightly clenched eyes were a wonder in themselves. Noah had given her every imaginable type of orgasm during their time together, but nothing had compared to this. As her mind was rocketing through space, there was a part of her convinced if they lived together for a hundred years, Noah would make every day better than the one before.

Chapter 26

NOAH HAD NO idea how he'd managed to stay on his feet. The power of his release had nearly blown apart every fiber of his being. Leaning over Ilaina with his cock still buried inside her, he felt a sense of satisfaction settle over him like a well-worn quilt. When he finally got his breathing under control, he maneuvered the two of them into the shower. Once they'd cleaned up, he planned to tuck Ilaina against him and enjoy a short nap wrapped in each other's arms.

When he woke up before she did, he leaned down and kissed her slightly rounded belly and whispered, "Be nice to your sweet mama you two, she is the light of my life."

He hadn't planned to mention her grandmother's words and didn't realize she was awake until he looked up and saw her watching him. She looked deeply into his eyes and asked, "*Shimasani* or Mitch?"

"*Níyol*," was all he'd said before he saw the tears in her eyes. "*Cara?* Talk to me, my love." His heart felt like it was in a vice. He couldn't imagine what on earth had put those tears in her dark eyes.

"I'm just overcome with joy. I've had so many blessings in my life, it seems almost selfish to be given yet another. To have you as the father of one child was a gift straight from the Great Spirit, but to be given two children is just…"

He hadn't let her finish before he silenced her with his kiss. She deserved every blessing she'd ever been given, and he planned to spend the rest of his life making sure she understood just how much.

It was almost three hours later when Noah escorted a much more rested Ilaina through the doors of the Climax Medical Center. Making their way to the large waiting room was slow going because it seemed almost every member of their small community was present. There were pink and blue balloons everywhere, and everyone seemed to be chattering a mile a minute. Looking down at Ilaina, he just chuckled at her wide-eyed stare.

"Too late to change your mind now, my love." He really was just kidding and certainly hadn't wanted to trigger her tears. When she seemed to take a step back from the crowd in fear, he turned her, so she was facing him. "Baby, what's this about? These are your friends."

Fear was coming off her in waves, and he had no idea why. Just then, he looked up and saw Mitch standing directly behind Ilaina and saw him nod to the side. Stepping back into the hall with Ilaina, he let Mitch lead them down the long corridor to a much smaller and more private waiting area.

Noticing how visibly pale she was, Noah settled her on the sofa before taking her trembling hand in his. Mitch sat down on the other side of Ilaina and looked at her for several seconds before speaking.

"Ilaina, I have a distinct advantage here because I'm able to hear your fears, but honey, your husband is baffled and very worried about you. Would you like some help to explain this?"

Baffled didn't begin to describe the soul-deep confusion

and worry Noah was experiencing. Mitch might think this was helping but *not so much*. Deciding to keep quiet and see where this led, Noah simply kept her hand in his and waited. She stared at Mitch for long seconds before she nodded her head slowly.

"Okay, as I'm sure Noah has taught you, shaking or nodding are not ordinarily acceptable answers, but I'm going to make an exception right now because I know right where your head is, and I want this put to rest quickly." Mitch smiled at Ilaina, and Noah noticed his friend had his hand gently wrapped around her wrist. Knowing the former SEAL was monitoring his wife's heart rate was oddly comforting.

"Now, you spent several years constantly being on guard in crowds because so often the people around you had little or no respect for your personal boundaries and continually made unreasonable demands, am I getting it about right?" When she nodded again, he smiled and continued, "If I say anything that's off-base, please don't hesitate to stop me, alright?" Again, she nodded, and Noah suddenly wished he could hear what Mitch was listening to so intently.

"I know you don't understand why this has happened today of all days, but I've worked with a lot of victims who have experienced various types of trauma over the years, sweetness, and I've seen a huge range of triggers for fears someone thought had been laid to rest. And pregnancy hormones amplify a lot of feelings, so you'll have to be extra diligent to allow your Dom to shelter and protect you.

"You can trust Noah to keep you safe, Ilaina, and you have a whole community of people out there who will step between you and danger without even blinking. You aren't alone anymore, but it will take a bit for your heart to catch up with what your mind already knows. Don't expect it to happen overnight and don't think this will be the last time you'll face this sort of challenge. But I promise you, it will be much easier next time." Noah watched as Mitch's eyes never left Alaina's face while he waited for her to process his words.

"How did you know?" Ilaina's words were so softly spoken, at first, Noah wasn't sure he'd heard correctly, but when Mitch smiled, he knew she had actually spoken the words.

"Well, to be honest, some of it just stood to reason. I've been working with victims for a long time, and some things are very predictable, particularly when you add that little hormone cocktail you'll be basking in for the next few months. Congratulations, by the way. They are going to be amazing children, and I'm so glad we'll all have each other for support when our own children are driving us mad."

Clay Red Cloud burst in the room at that moment and pulled Ilaina to her feet, twirled her around in his arms before setting her feet back on the floor.

"Come on, Aunt Lainy. You have a new nephew, and he's *wailing* to meet you."

Noah saw his wife sway a bit and knew she was likely dizzy from being spun around so quickly, so he stood and wrapped his arm around her shoulders, starting to lead her out of the room, but she turned back to Mitch and wrapped her arms around his waist and hugged him tightly.

"Thank you very much, Mitch. I appreciate your help more than you know, and I'll be sure to tell Rissa what a lucky woman she is."

"You do that sweetness. Bryant and I both keep telling

her that same thing, but maybe she'll listen to *you*." Mitch chuckled before turning her back to Noah. "Now, you need to go meet your new nephew and don't be afraid to open your heart Ilaina, there are a lot of people who will happily walk through the fire with you."

NOAH LEANED AGAINST the wall of the Lamonts' large family room, watching the scene play out before him. It had been six weeks since the chaos surrounding the births of Alexa Kathleen Lamont, Matthew Saul Bartell, and James Lane Red Cloud. The decision to combine their christenings had been a blessing for Noah because he'd been able to take close to a thousand pictures in just a few hours rather than spreading it out over several days.

The babies had cooperated—hell, he'd even gained the cooperation of all three of the Lamont triplets *at the same time*, something their parents assured him was unheard of—but the most photogenic woman in the room was still his sweet *Cara*.

Watching as Ilaina rocked her nephew as he rested on her rapidly growing belly, Noah thought back over the time he'd spent over the past couple of weeks training former FBI agents Derek Lake and Joe Rivera. The two would be leaving soon on a mission with ShadowDance's second female operative, former special prosecutor, Brianna Francis. Teaching the two male agents to take passable photos had been easy, teaching them how to interact as if they were a couple had proven to be much more difficult.

When a tip had come in about Brianna's younger sister

Tiffani, who had been kidnapped from the University of Texas campus almost two years ago, Brianna had pushed for the FBI to investigate. They had stonewalled, so she called the Lamonts. Alex had already been recruiting former SEALS Lake and Rivera, and when they'd heard about Brianna being put off by the agency they were currently working for, they hadn't hesitated to walk away.

Noah had watched as the three of them fought their almost magnetic attraction to one another and wondered how long they would continue to try to fool themselves. He couldn't help the chuckle that escaped at the thought about how pointless it was to fight fate.

Raising the camera he was holding and zooming in on Ilaina to take several shots as she leaned down to kiss Jamie's forehead, Noah was overwhelmed with a sense of love for her and the children she carried. When she looked up and caught his eye, the sweet smile that spread over her face was perfect, and he was grateful his camera had been ready to capture the moment.

When Ilaina stood and walked over to return the baby to his mother, Noah glanced at the last shot he'd just taken. What he saw almost dropped him to his knees. The light had danced through the floor to ceiling windows highlighting Ilaina in a way that made her appear to have angel wings.

Another perfect picture…

BOOKS BY AVERY GALE

The ShadowDance Club
Katarina's Return – Book One
Jenna's Submission – Book Two
Rissa's Recovery – Book Three
Trace & Tori – Book Four
Reborn as Bree – Book Five
Red Clouds Dancing – Book Six
Perfect Picture – Book Seven

Club Isola
Capturing Callie – Book One
Healing Holly – Book Two
Claiming Abby – Book Three

Masters of the Prairie Winds Club
Out of the Storm
Saving Grace
Jen's Journey
Bound Treasure
Punishing for Pleasure
Accidental Trifecta
Missionary Position
Another Second Chance
Star-Crossed Miracles
Dusted Star
Lilly's Choice

The Wolf Pack Series
Mated – Book One
Fated Magic – Book Two
Tempted by Darkness – Book Three

The Knights of the Boardroom
Book One
Book Two
Book Three

The Morgan Brothers of Montana
Coral Hearts – Book One
Dancing with Deception – Book Two
Caged Songbird – Book Three
Game On – Book Four
Well Bred – Book Five

Mountain Mastery
Well Written
Savannah's Sentinel
Sheltering Reagan

Enchanted Holidays
The Christmas Painting

I would love to hear from you!

Website:
www.averygale.com

Facebook:
facebook.com/avery.gale.3

Twitter:
@avery_gale